Mac in the City of Light

The words of the prophet

Mac in the City of Light

Christopher Ward

DUNDURN
TORONTO

Editor: Allister Thompson
Design: Courtney Horner
Printer: Webcom

Library and Archives Canada Cataloguing in Publication

Ward, Christopher
        Mac in the city of light / Christopher Ward.

Issued also in electronic formats.
ISBN 978-1-4597-0614-9

        I. Title.

PS8645.A71M33 2013   jC813'.6   C2012-903210-7

1   2   3   4   5   17   16   15   14   13

We acknowledge the support of the **Canada Council for the Arts** and the **Ontario Arts Council** for our publishing program. We also acknowledge the financial support of the **Government of Canada** through the **Canada Book Fund** and **Livres Canada Books**, and the **Government of Ontario** through the **Ontario Book Publishing Tax Credit** and the **Ontario Media Development Corporation**.

Care has been taken to trace the ownership of copyright material used in this book. The author and the publisher welcome any information enabling them to rectify any references or credits in subsequent editions.

J. Kirk Howard, President

Printed and bound in Canada.

Visit us at
Dundurn.com
Definingcanada.ca
@dundurnpress
Facebook.com/dundurnpress

Dundurn	Gazelle Book Services Limited	Dundurn
3 Church Street, Suite 500	White Cross Mills	2250 Military Road
Toronto, Ontario, Canada	High Town, Lancaster, England	Tonawanda, NY
M5E 1M2	LA1 4XS	U.S.A. 14150

To
Rachel Mackenzie, the original "Mac,"
for the inspiration
Robin for the joy of adventure
and Mom and Dad for the love of reading

One

"It's summer in Paris. You can't wear only sneakers!" My mom pleadingly held up a pair of lemon-coloured sandals for inspection as my dad peered into a stack of guidebooks.

"It's a school walking tour, Mom, not tea at the Ritz ... and besides, my ankle's still a bit swollen." I instantly regretted reminding her of last week's "incident," when I'd tied some sheets together and parachuted off their bedroom balcony.

"Did you realize that the Erik Satie museum in Paris, celebrating the famous twentieth-century composer, is the smallest in the world?" My dad hummed an obscure melody, bouncing his head lightly from side to side. "Oh, but it's by appointment only."

I feigned disappointment as my mom launched a chiffon offensive. "And this picks up your eyes beautifully," she said, wrapping something caramel-coloured and more than a little itchy around my neck. "How I envy you, sipping a coupe of champagne ... or rather, a Shirley Temple at the Café de Flore in the very heart of the artistic *milieu* on Boulevard St. Germain." At this she became a little dreamy, and I saw my chance to tuck the sandals back in the closet with the scarf and floral frocks.

"Hey sweetie, did you know that they still leave roses daily on the grave of the little sparrow, Edith Piaf, at the Père Lachaise cemetery?" He sang her famous song, "La Vie en Rose," in a fluty falsetto as he waltzed my mom around the bedroom.

While they were distracted, I put seven of every item of clothing I'd need in my backpack, along with my copy of Victor Hugo's *Notre Dame de Paris*, number one on our summer reading list, and snapped it shut. "Okay. Done."

"Don't forget this." My dad handed me the letter from his old friend and former bandmate, Rudee Daroo. "It takes some time to catch on to Rudee-speak, but he'll give you a great cab driver's view of Paris." Rudee, a classically trained organist, had toured with my dad's band one summer way back before they had computers. My mom loves the scrapbook, which features pictures of my dad with a ponytail and a mushroom-embroidered vest. Rudee was the resident clown who had supposedly once played a keyboard solo with his nose and with his feet in the air. Other tales of his love for pickled herring juice and beets always seem to bring choruses of laughter, but I guess that's just adult humour. The letter looked like someone had served dinner on it.

Hey Mr. Bigsport,
Good to hear from you after so many spin cycles. How are you and the pretty missus? So you are air mailing the little Mac to Paris to smell some buildings. Good — I understand architexture you know.

Me — I'm fine. No, I'm not. I've got a problem and I don't know what it is. It's Sashay. She says her gig at the Moulin D'Or is in danger and it's the only place she can dance and that when this one ends she's going to do one last twirl and disappear. And there is something strange about the city but I'm not going to tell you because no one believes me and you already think I'm mad as a dormitory.

Nevermind. Send the sprout to the Pont Neuf when I go on my brakes at 4. Jerome the bookseller will find me.
Yours for days, Rudee

My mom watched with trembling lips as we got in the car to pick up my friend Penelope on the way to the airport. I was glad that Mom was off to "Twigs and Roots," her annual yoga retreat in the hills near Santa Barbara. Mellow is good for moms.

My dad called from the driver's seat, "Okay, let's go, Mac, or as they say in France, '*allez-oop*'!"

The "Mac" is short for Mackenzie. My mom is a teacher and my dad is a songwriter, and we live in California in Upper Mandeville, which tells you that there's a Lower Mandeville. Both towns are made up of wood-and-brick houses that run the length of a very green canyon, not far from the ocean. Sycamore trees surround our house. The teetering redwood fence has ruby-coloured bougainvillea climbing over it, and my mom has planted roses and calla lilies all around the property. There are lots of creatures that share the place with us — hummingbirds, lizards, dragonflies, deer, the odd skunk, and even the occasional bobcat.

I like Upper Mandeville. It's a little quieter, not as ritzy as Lower Mandeville, where my friend Penelope lives. The trees meet over the road, and it's easier to get lost, which I like to do whenever I can, and it has more butterflies.

When we passed through the gates and pulled up in front of Penelope's house, she rolled out her matching set of pink Louis Vuitton luggage in top international girly-girl form, lowered her giant sunglasses and flicked a tiny wave in the direction of her parents. "*Au revoir, maman, papa* ... Paris awaits." Inside the car, she snapped her first of a million photos, me cross-eyed, pretending to read Victor Hugo upside down.

Two

Airport. Waiting room. Plane. Luggage. Customs. Bus. Paris!!!

Most of a day and almost 6,000 miles later, I stood with Penelope and ten other girls from my advanced French class outside the student residence in the Latin Quarter that was to be our home for the next week. A stream of taxis and a blustery wind swept down the ancient boulevard. The whole street resembled one giant café. We didn't manage the "two straight lines" thing, but it still reminded me of an American version of Madeline and her posse. The school chaperone handed us off, a little too hastily, I thought, and disappeared into a nearby *brasserie* for the first *café crème* of the rest of her life. Our Parisian tour guide, Mademoiselle Lesage, batted her eyelashes like Audrey Hepburn and spoke in a bird-like trill.

"*Les filles. Les filles!* Girls! *Bienvenue*, welcome to Paris. Before we check you into your rooms, I want to say how excited I am to guide you on your architectural tour of the beauties of Paris. From the gothic majesty of Notre Dame to the breathtaking modernity of I.M. Pei's Louvre pyramid, we shall see it all...."

"Those hand gestures look like she's making doves fly out of a hat," I whispered, and Penelope bit her lip. I checked my watch and realized I was going to have to sneak away soon if I was going to meet Rudee on time.

"... and the Renaissance creations that honour Marie de Medici, the Italian wife of Henry IV, whose sculpture is featured on the Pont Neuf...."

"Excuse me," I interrupted, "Mademoiselle Lesage, is the Pont Neuf near here?"

"*Oui*, it's but a few minutes walk along the *quai*," she replied, gesturing vaguely toward the river. "But why do you ask?"

"Oh, it's just that, you know ... Henry and Marie ... I'm a big fan of the reno at the Louvre."

She continued with a puzzled expression. "And who could ignore the baroque glory of Louis XIV, the 'Sun King,' whose vision for the incomparable 'Les Invalides' was inspired, they say, by St. Peter's in Rome."

"Penelope, can you cover for me if I slip away for a few hours?"

"No problem," she said, "when she's taking attendance, I'll just put on a beret, go to the other side of the group and look restless."

"Ha-ha, and thanks," I said, giving Penelope a little hug. Mademoiselle Lesage seemed to be just warming up.

"... and the tiny little oval windows known as '*oeil de boeuf,*' which means ... anyone?" she paused hopefully, "eye of the beef, of course."

Three

As the wind picked up, so did the pedestrians' pace along the Quai des Grand Augustins (no just plain Elm Street here); I hustled along with the crowd, my backpack bouncing behind me. Looking over the wall to the River Seine below, I saw barges and tourist boats passing under bridges and kids with guitars taking shelter ahead of what felt like a coming storm. Booksellers unravelled plastic wrap over tables of books and posters. Just beyond them I spotted a beautiful old bridge with stone half-moon shapes on it and a statue of a man on a horse.

"A little lost, *ma petite*?" A bookseller who looked as old as the bridge itself called out to me. At that moment the sky opened, and a wild rain crashed down upon us. He quickly began closing up his bookstall. "Here, you'll need this today," he said and handed me a tattered umbrella with the head of a duck on the wooden handle.

"Thank you," I said and struggled to open it as the wind tried to gather me up. "Who is the statue of and what bridge is this?"

He pulled his coat around his neck and continued closing his stall. "That's Henri the Fourth, one of the great kings of France, and this is the Pont Neuf." He smiled at me through a bushy white beard. "That means 'new bridge,' although it's actually not so new; it was built about four hundred years ago. It's the oldest bridge in Paris."

A rivulet of rain slipped through a hole in the umbrella and ran unnoticed down my face. I must have looked a bit like a statue myself.

"C'mon, I don't want you to catch a cold on your first day in France, little one. Rudee's waiting at the cabstand. It's Mac, isn't it? I'm Jerome."

There was only one taxi idling at the corner, and in the time it took the bookseller and me to reach it, the driver had waved away a businessman with his briefcase on top of his head and a tourist couple trying to stuff a wad of bills through the crack in the window.

Jerome tapped at the cab window and leaned in to speak with the driver, who turned to look at me intensely.

"Good luck, Mademoiselle Mac," Jerome said as he waved and disappeared into the rainy street.

The door was barely closed before the cab took off over the Pont Neuf. I think I would have felt safer on the back of Henri the Fourth's horse.

Four

The taxi was filled with seriously gloomy organ music, and a deodorizer in the shape of a beet dangled from the ashtray. In the mirror, a pair of stormy eyes glared at me from under a forehead that resembled the edge of a cliff. Over the seat, which was covered in those little wooden balls you only ever see in a taxi, I could make out a helmet of hair wedged on an otherwise bald head that I recognized from my dad's scrapbook as belonging to Rudee Daroo. I smiled and a voice growled from the front seat, "Who pushed the funny button?"

"My name is Mac, and my dad ..."

"Yesyesyes, I know him well, and why you were not here yesterday is not worth the sound of the clock."

I felt like I needed a translator, but I pressed on. "I did *leave* yesterday, Rudee, but it's an overnight flight, so you see ..." I realized why he might have expected me the day before, "… anyway, my dad told me all about you and the band, and he played me the tapes of the Pipeline Tour and the nose solo …"

Rudee snorted and turned down a narrow street, squeezing past a double-decker tourist bus. "Don't make me smoke out loud. I should send you straight home, but the least I can do is give you a bowl of borscht."

Borscht wasn't my first choice, but I was very hungry. Rudee turned up the organ music till the doors rattled, so I sat back and got my first look at the old stone wonders of Paris on a rainy day. He navigated the taxi down an impossibly narrow alley and into a vine-covered shed before leading the way, grumbling to himself, into the shadow of a gloriously beautiful church with three spires, two of which were topped with gleaming gold crosses. It seemed ancient and dream-like to me. We rushed into a side entrance and up a set of stairs to a small apartment with two tiny rooms. Shelves of cracked dishes, plastic flowers, a stopped clock, and an intense odour of cooking vegetables greeted me.

The source of the smell that hung in the air like a damp towel was soon revealed as Rudee starting warming his pot of borscht, stirring happily and whistling some sombre little melody.

"Rudee, where are we?" I asked.

"The Église Russe, the Russian church where I play the organ every Sunday, little quarter note. The taxi is just to make ends meet during the week. Here you go."

He placed a bowl of purple steam in front of me with the first smile I had seen from him, and I was glad for both. A plate of bread with a crust like concrete, but soft inside, helped the beets go down. "Listen, I'm sorry for being upset. I thought I had misplaced you, and I've been sweating marbles since yesterday, but ... so, your daddy played you 'Back Burner,' did he?"

I nodded and he seemed pleased. While I ate, he told me some of the history of the Église Russe, including the fact that Picasso had gotten married there, and all about some music composers from behind what he called the "Cabbage Curtain." He asked if I had noticed that one of the crosses was missing from the spire in the middle of the church and told me sadly about the recent theft. By the time Rudee got to his version of the immortal Pipeline Tour, I was feeling a bit woozy.

"Okokok, little Mac, you need to count some winks, I can see. You can stay in the turret tonight, and we'll get you back to your class tomorrow."

I was too weak to argue, so he grabbed my backpack and led me up a wooden staircase with no railing into a spire of the church. The air seemed different, fragrant but older and definitely dustier. The first thing I noticed by the light of the candle that Rudee left burning was the stained glass windows. They had panels like a comic book of saints and kings and queens, plus a lot of people in robes and hoods. I'm not sure how a full-sized person could sleep on the wooden bed that was attached to one wall and followed the curve of the church tower. There was a sparse library of very heavy-looking books. The corners of the bookshelves were tiny carved angels that seemed to guard the bed. Who had they looked down on and protected before me, I wondered. I didn't feel as sleepy as I should have, so I pulled out the smallest book I could find from the shelf. It still felt like a box of bricks. Inside were paintings of a beautiful church like this one and winding streets filled with food carts, dogs, and children playing.

Five

I woke to coloured light dancing across my bed. The windows came to life in the morning sun, pale as it was. When I pulled the shutters open, I felt dizzy for a moment. The city of Paris spilled out in front of my eyes — ancient buildings with balconies jammed full of geraniums and a thousand miniature chimneys that sat like broken teeth on a comb. Everywhere were people stopping to talk, gesturing dramatically, buying breakfast, eating as they walked, stepping around pigeons, rushing along dragging children behind them, reading on bicycles, carrying little dogs in baskets and purses or inside their coats. There were the famous monuments I had seen in my school books — the golden dome of Les Invalides, the Eiffel Tower, Sacre Coeur, and the River Seine winding like a ribbon across it all.

I bounced down the staircase to find that Rudee had left me some crusty bread, tiny oranges, savagely stinky cheese, and a map of the city. A note on the torn corner of a newspaper said *Gone to work — have some times*. I descended the stairs from his room and passed through the garden and into the street.

Everything was different. The noises, the voices, the shops, and the people of Paris — the wrinkled roadmap face of the chestnut vendor, leaning over his fire, pushing a few blackened chestnuts around — no, *merci*. He looked as old as time. And the children — the babies were like the dolls in the toy stores I saw everywhere, the ones having tea in the window. Penelope must be in heaven.

Thinking of Penelope reminded me that I'd better make my way to the Latin Quarter to meet my class. I followed the right bank and crossed the river on the Pont Des Arts, a beautiful pedestrian bridge that was decorated with an exhibit of wacky collage photographs. I arrived, a little out of breath, to see the tour group assembled on the sidewalk in front of our residence.

Penelope spotted me and whispered immediately, "Nice timing, Mac. While we've been waiting for you to emerge from your *chambre*, which I don't believe you've actually seen, Mademoiselle Lesage's sympathy for your newfound allergy to almond paste has been wearing thin."

Our tour guide rushed over to me and put her hand on my forehead. "*Mon Dieu*, child, but you are so warm." Over her shoulder, I saw Penelope fanning herself dramatically.

"I do feel a little faint, Mademoiselle Lesage," I said feebly.

"*Oui*, I can see that. Penelope told me you had a reaction to the almond croissant at breakfast."

"Yes, I had no idea it had ... almonds in it."

She looked at me pityingly. "Well, Mac, I'm going to have to insist that you remain in your room. We have so much walking to do today."

I tried not to laugh at Penelope's giant "ahhh" expression. "I suppose you know best." As Mademoiselle Lesage herded the girls toward Boulevard St. Michel, I made my way into the lobby. While giving them a head start, I glanced at the daily paper, *Le Devoir*, which announced a big "Lighten Up" celebration at the Arc de Triomphe. I *did* have some monuments to see.

I hustled alongside the river past the Musée D'Orsay. Check. Crossing the river on the Pont de la Concorde, I whizzed by the Grand Palais and the Petit Palais. Check. Check. Wow, Monuments R Us here.

I soon found myself on the widest street I'd ever seen. The Champs Élysées was abuzz with what looked like bumper cars, and the broad sidewalks were filled with people speaking every language imaginable. As I approached the Arc de Triomphe, I saw a crowd and heard music. I slipped through the bodies for a closer look. There was a band playing on a temporary stage decorated with plastic palm trees that had trunks shaped like the Eiffel Tower. A banner read LIGHTEN UP PARIS! in bright orange letters. The band was in full swing with dancers and coordinated back-up singers and a skinny little vocalist who was about three-quarters man and one-quarter hair. He wore a gold cape and puss-in-boots shoes with buckles. His back-up singers wore matching outfits in different colours, each representing a suit of cards as they dipped, turned, and spun like a machine. The dancers, dressed in *fleur de lis* bikinis, were shaking their hips like little dogs trying to dry off.

The singer was singing, "Shaaaade ... quit giving me shade, baby."

The back-up singers did one final cake-mixer spin and landed in front of their mikes, singing, "You're raining on my parade," as the music abruptly halted.

The dancers produced twirling umbrellas that spun to a blur, lifting them off the stage into the afternoon for a dazzling crowd-pleasing finish.

The singer remained on stage, and as the applause faded, he announced, "Ladies and gentlemen, mesdames et messieurs, please give a warm, and I mean warm welcome to the prefect of Paris, Luc Fiat!"

A man bounced up the steps, took the microphone, and waved to the cheering crowd. He wore a dazzling white suit with a golden sun emblazoned on the shoulders and rays extending down the back and sleeves. He wore silver cowboy boots and mirrored sunglasses in the shape of little suns. He smiled a long, thin, crescent smile that looked like it had drawstrings at the corners.

"Yessss. Ouiiiii. Merccci!"

He stretched out the words and nodded approvingly at the crowd.

"Today is a special day for all Parisians. Today we say '*non*' to the grey clouds and 'pooh' to the rain. We will borrow a cup of California and a hint of Hawaii to scare away the grey. Today, my fellow citizens, we lighten up!"

At this, a screen unfurled behind him showing the Seine and one of the tourist boats, the *bateau mouche*. The crowd ooo'd as the dancers from the band sailed by on orange water-skis, waving, smiling, still holding their little parasols.

At the other end of the Champs Élysées, in the Place de la Concorde, fireworks went off in the shape of a giant happy face. A small plane was busily spelling out the words "Lighten Up." The crowd seemed enthralled as Luc Fiat pointed toward the happy face that was melting to the ground and shouted, "It's up to you, *mes amis*, to lighten up old Paris."

He bounded off the stage as quickly as he had arrived, down a set of stairs toward the backstage area. I noticed, almost hidden behind the screen, two identical characters in long black trench coats, faces hidden by their fedora hats with the glow of cigarettes the only sign of life. The coats seemed to billow like smoke as they parted a backstage curtain to allow Luc Fiat to exit before they followed right behind. Curious, I eased through the dispersing crowd and pushed apart a couple of wooden barriers. I peeked inside a large tent. At that precise moment, Fiat turned to look back and briefly caught my eye.

He registered surprise but quickly disappeared into the folds of heavy grey material. Then I heard a voice that sounded like it came from a barrel.

"Nice work, Monsieur Fiat, you got the touch," followed by a deep laugh.

A thin voice hissed in reply, "Oh shut up, Scar, and help me down."

I tried to slow my pounding heart as I heard a scraping, accompanied by a damp, fishy smell. The voices echoed then suddenly stopped. I eased around a tent flap and into the back as my eyes got used to the dark. Nothing. No one. How could that be? There was only one way out. I walked around, and all I saw was a couple of cigarette butts ground out beside a manhole cover.

"Can I help you?" a man asked, putting his hand on my shoulder, making me jump about a foot in the air. He was carrying a broom and wearing a "City of Paris LIGHTEN UP!" sweatshirt.

"No," I replied, wondering what I was doing there anyway. "I just wanted to meet Monsieur Fiat, that's all," I blurted.

He smiled and nodded. "Let me help you find your way out, mademoiselle. I don't think anyone actually meets Luc Fiat, at least not with those two giant bookends that always follow him around standing in the way."

On my way back to Rudee's, I thought I'd sample a guacamole croissant at one of the stands set up on the Champs Élysées. It wasn't very good. Or maybe I wasn't very hungry.

Six

Back at the Russian church, Rudee was in his room, stirring something purple and foamy on his little burner. Nearby sat an open jar of pickled herring and a fork. He wiped the corner of his mouth. "Hungry, little one?"

"No," I lied. The walk home had made me realize how famished I was, but then the aroma of Rudee's room quickly took care of that. I told him about the rally. He brightened and said, "Now, this is what we need. I tried to drive by, but I couldn't get close; I saw the happy head firecracker. You know, Paris has been looking darker to me lately, and anything that can polish our eyes is good."

I felt like I was starting to understand him. I tried to tell him about Luc Fiat's bodyguards and his odd disappearance, but Rudee seemed more interested in the contents of his pot. I climbed the staircase to my attic room and was watching the sun ease down over the chimneys and church spires, changing everything into rosy silhouettes when Rudee called up to me, "Hey, American shrimplette, do you want to come with me to take Sashay to the club?"

I didn't have time to ask who or where, because he was heading loudly down the stairs. As I grabbed my sweatshirt, it occurred to me that Rudee seemed to have forgotten about sending me back to my school group. Penelope would be more than curious as to where I was, but I knew she'd cover for me. I followed him through the church garden to the shed where his cab was waiting. We backed down the vine-covered alley and into the cobblestone street. Rudee changed the lighting in his cab from purple to a soft gold and was fishing through a box of tapes under the seat as he navigated the traffic. He muttered to himself till he found what he was looking for.

"Rudee?" I felt like I was interrupting some ritual.

"Sorry, little one, I forgot you were here."

"Who's Sashay?"

He slowly turned his head to stare at me, wordlessly at first. His normally pointy brow seemed to arch out even further from his face, making his eyes look like they were staring out at me from inside a pair of caves. "Didn't your daddy tell you anything? Sashay D'Or, *la reine des rêves*, the queen of dreams, the most enchanting woman in all of Parisian nightlife, you know nothing about? Ah, Sashay...."

Rudee seemed to glaze over for a moment, with a distant, almost sad expression. "Sorry, Mac, where was I? Sashay, of course. She knows ways of taking people away with that swirly girl dance of hers. You remember things ..." his voice trailed off before the fire in it returned, "... she was the toast of all Paris. Now she works for people who don't appreciate her. No one does ... like I do."

At this moment the radio cut in with a burst of static. "Fifty-two. *Cinquante-deux*. Are you there?"

Rudee grabbed his microphone. "*Oui*, I'm here after all."

"Rudee, you little cockroach, *ça va*?" A crusty female voice came from the speaker.

"Yes, *oui*, Madeleine, you old sea hag, *ça va*."

A cackling laugh, part static, part cough, shot back, "I've got a new recipe for curing baldness, *mon ami*."

"Really?" Rudee sounded cautious but interested.

"Listen, take equal parts goose liver and very ripe brie and let it sit beside your bed for one month. Then spread it on your head and sit under a lamp for six hours, and do not move."

Rudee was taking notes while driving.

"And the next morning, my shiny-domed driver, you'll have a full head of hair."

"That's it?" Rudee couldn't hide the hope in his voice.

"Oh, just one last thing. You need ... one very gullible bald cabbie."

A chorus of laughter echoed over the radio. Rudee turned the colour of his beet stew and slammed down the handset.

At this point we swung into a narrow street and stopped in front of a darkened storefront that read "Musée D'Écharpe." I'd never heard of a scarf museum. Could Erik Satie's place be smaller than this? On the floor above, a curtain parted slightly then closed, and the lights went out. Rudee jumped out of the cab, opened the back door, and stood waiting while a woman whisked from between the buildings and into the back seat. I turned to get my first look at the "queen of dreams." I could barely focus on her face for the wild profusion of hair and scarves in the dim golden glow of Rudee's cab.

"Sashay, this is ..." began Rudee.

"Mac," she said in a whisper, "*enchanté*," and extended a hand contained in a silky glove that travelled far up her sleeve.

"Hi," was all I could manage as her eyes, located deep beneath waxy lashes, found mine.

Before we could go any further, Rudee hit the gas and pulled away, pushing "play" and filling the cab with the sound of a velvety male singer. In the mirror, Sashay looked like she was somewhere else. Rudee said nothing, so I thought I'd better do the same. We eased through the streets of St. Germain till we approached a cluster of cars and people standing in groups dressed for a night on the town, laughing and talking happily. On one side of a narrow passage, I could see the lights of the club gleaming on the polished steel and stone exterior. The sign read MOULIN D'OR and below it was a poster of Sashay surrounded by lights looking like she had just emerged from a silver cloud. The groups parted as we slowly drove past the entrance then stopped in front of an alley leading to the side of the building. Above a dimly lit doorway, I could just make out a sign that read STAGE DOOR. Sashay departed without a word and went in.

There was a man in a long black coat in the shadows by the door, standing very still. I might not have noticed him if it weren't for the glow of the cigarette under the brim of his hat.

Seven

"There goes the most beautiful woman to have ever taken the stage in Paris or anywhere with curtains," sighed Rudee as we drove away, "you can have your Coco LaFoie, your Tipi Chaussette."

My mind was still on the smoking man by the stage door, but I could see that this was not the moment to mention it to Rudee. Another set of rain-slicked cobblestone streets later, we arrived at a café. Every car outside, all parked at odd angles to the curb, was a taxi. The blinking sign in the window of the smoky room said CAF TA; then I saw that with the burned-out letters lit up, it would have spelled CAFE TAXI. It was packed, bright, and very loud, and the smell of coffee and fresh pastry ruled. In one corner, someone was getting a shave and a haircut. Card playing, arm wrestling, and arguing contributed to the chaos. As Rudee looked for a table, he was spotted by some friends.

"Hey, Rudee, I've got some goose liver for you."

"Did you bring the brie?"

The laughter was punctuated by more voices. "Hey, who's that? Have you given up on the most beautiful woman to have ever taken the stage?"

"Business slow, Monsieur Rudee? Doing a little babysitting on the side?"

That was it for me. I stood up on a chair and shouted above the crowd, "He's not my babysitter. Rudee's my friend!"

This was greeted by some good-natured "ooolalas" and "wellwellwells," and the crowd moved back to their drinks and on to other matters. Rudee looked the most surprised of all by my outburst. A tall, thin driver with a mop of hair escaping from a pork pie hat and a nose that looked like it could slice bread was waving at us and pointing to a couple of empty chairs. We sat down, and Rudee introduced me to François Caboche.

"Friend of Rudee's is a friend of mine." He grinned through a wispy moustache that hung like a curtain over his mouth. "Call me Dizzy."

He saw my expression and went on. "No, it's not a balance problem; my mom was in love with Dizzy Bluebird, and when he toured here with his hot half dozen, she was at every gig. She put a mini trombone into my hands when I was in the crib." Dizzy tilted his head at Rudee. "Your pal Rudee's a heckuva fine organist, you know. We jam on Saturdays upstairs; you want to come by?" Rudee didn't jump in, so I just smiled.

I said my dad had told me all about Rudee's talents. "He played me the Pipeline Tour tapes. He said Rudee's solo in 'Strange Glove' should be studied by every kid who wants to call himself an organist."

Rudee couldn't hide his pride and asked if I'd heard my dad's vocal on "Transatlantic Train." I didn't tell him it just sounded totally weird to me.

"Listen, Rudee." Dizzy lowered his voice so it could barely be heard above the din of CAFTA and leaned toward his friend. "I've been thinking about what you said about the city getting darker, and I'm sorry that I laughed at you, *mon ami*. I know the theft of the cross from the Église Russe bothers you a lot, and I figured that's what was getting to you. Anyway, I was picking up my usual fare on Rue Bonaparte, and I realized that I couldn't read the building numbers. There was no fog, the lamps were on, but it seemed a bit darker to me. Maybe we're both crazy."

"That's it, slideman," Rudee burst in excitedly then quickly glanced around the room to see if anyone was paying attention before continuing. "I know it's true. Paris is getting darker by the day. Hardly but slowly. A driver in the Métro drove past the Pigalle station and two hundred passengers on the platform yesterday."

Rudee paid for the drinks and the warm chocolate croissants that had magically appeared and quickly disappeared, and we all headed into the street. We waved to Dizzy, who got into a very low-slung cab with exhaust pipes that looked like trombones. His cab belched blue smoke, and Rudee shook his head. "Only bohemians would travel like this."

The café door swung open, and a driver wider than the doorway squeezed out to spit in the street. Spotting us, he lumbered over.

"Daroo, you lunatic, how do you afford gas with all your freeloading friends?" He snorted like a pit bull and tilted his face close to mine. When he spoke, his breath could've been used as rust remover. "Past your bedtime, isn't it, nana?"

Rudee stepped between us. "Her name is Mac, sewer lips. Isn't it time for your big flea bath?"

This gross chunk of man lifted Rudee off the ground with one hand and dangled him like a dirty sock. "I think you need a new hinge for that hairdo of yours, beet breath. Sorry you'll miss the show at the club tonight."

Rudee's eyes seemed to recede under his mighty brow, but he said nothing. His assailant dropped him to the pavement and strode off, laughing to himself and spitting like a broken faucet.

Once he was out of sight, Rudee gathered himself and said, "Blag LeBoeuf. I've known him since we were knee high to fire hydrants.

"Our families knew each other from the old country. Then we went apelove for the same girl, don't you know." He shrugged, and a small smile emerged. "He lost the girl to me, and it's been like this ever since."

I wanted to know more about Blag, but as soon as we settled into Rudee's cab and he adjusted the lights and music to his liking, the radio squawked, and Madeleine's voice cut through. "*Bonsoir,* everyone. Just thought you all should know that the cross from the domed church has been stolen. *Incroyable, non?* Let me know if you hear something, and I'll pass it along to the others."

"The domed church. That's Les Invalides," said Rudee in an awed tone. "That's where Napoleon is boxed. The church with the golden dome is one of Paris' most shining monuments. But how could someone ..."

He yanked the wheel of the cab to the left, and I fell onto his shoulder. He threaded the needle across six lanes of cars as he madly circled the Arc de Triomphe. "Sorry," he muttered. "I must see this for my ownself."

Eight

When we slammed to a stop outside the domed church, a TV crew was setting up hastily, uncoiling cables and mounting a camera on a tripod. A reporter was fixing her make-up and throwing her hair back for that windblown look. A small collection of blue-and-white police cars was gathered at the entrance, and official looking people were trying to appear busy. Rudee spotted someone, and they exchanged greetings.

"Magritte, *ça va?*" Rudee said to a well-tanned policeman in a bowler hat and tailored black coat smoking a pipe and pulling on a pair of gloves.

"Ah, my old friend," and tipping his hat at me, "mademoiselle, *enchanté*. Rudee, I cannot thank you enough for delivering the Picasso thief to me."

"He refused to pay the oversized baggage charge and ..." Rudee shrugged.

"Still, we are grateful ... now, tonight is a theft of another kind."

"Magritte, I can't believe it. First the cross of the Église Russe, and now this." Rudee looked like he would cry any second. "And not only the cross, but the dome, the beautiful frosted dome, painted black."

It was true; the freshly cropped dome was drenched in what looked like a bad paint job, still sticky and dripping on the windows below.

"*Oui*, I know, it is a travesty," Magritte said coolly, "and they chose matte instead of glossy, which serves to de-emphasize the Baroque influence of the concave flying buttresses...."

Rudee's impatience with this tangent was obvious. "But who, who, Magritte, and why?" he interrupted.

"Who, yes. Myself, I suspect a group of militant atheists from Montparnasse. But how, *mon ami*, that is the question. It was, if you will excuse a small joke, an outside job, because the entire building was locked and still is." Magritte shrugged, and we all looked up to where the magnificent dome now blended in with the night sky, with only a silhouette to distinguish it. "I must begin my investigation. If you'd like to walk with me...."

Rudee nodded, and we followed as Inspector Magritte dusted doors and windows with fingerprint powder, shone a flashlight into shrubs and down stairways that led to locked doors. He held a magnifying glass close to read the inscription on an ancient turquoise cannon as Rudee chatted with him. While they talked about the weight of crosses and discussed various theories as to how one could be raised and transported, I stared at the perfect crescent moon that lit up the immaculately designed gardens. The moonlight caught something shiny, so I walked over to a row of trees and picked up a pair of mirrored glasses. A chill ran from my hand to my spine.

"What have you there, mademoiselle?" asked Magritte, shining his light on my find. I started to hand them to him, but he curled up his nose. "*Non, merci*. Ah, the tourists. No taste at all you know, present company excepted, of course." He smiled at me. "How anyone could see through these, I don't know. Although I suppose to reflect back the absurdity of our existence on this ..."

Rudee coughed and said his goodbyes.

"Ah, it's *adieu* then, *mes amis*." Magritte waved and went back to his ruminations.

Back in the cab, Rudee looked at his watch. "Oh, *mon dieu*, we have to pick up Sashay; her show's almost over. He who hesitates is late."

We zoomed through the streets, now emptying of people. When we arrived at the Moulin D'Or, couples were spilling into the street, arm in arm, laughing and leaning on one another. A lone figure was the last to emerge.

"Rudee," I asked, "isn't that Blag LeBoeuf?" I hoped another encounter like the one outside CAFTA wasn't about to happen.

Rudee barely glanced. "No doubt, little one, he still comes to make eyelids at her after all this time, and the club ... his family ... well ..."

He left the thought unfinished, concentrating on navigating through the less than sure-footed crowd; but it was then that I understood whom they had fought over years ago.

We didn't have to wait long at the stage door. In a whoosh of scarves and in a long cream-coloured cape, Sashay materialized and was in the back seat before Rudee could even open his door.

"Let's go. Leave now. Please." She sank into the seat as we drove away. She didn't seem to notice that Rudee had been too surprised to turn off the organ music that poured like mud from the speakers. I leaned forward and switched off the sound. Rudee did the same with the taxi radio, and we travelled in silence. The only accompaniment was the soft swish of the tires over the rain-soaked streets as we made our way to Sashay's apartment. When we arrived and Rudee pulled up and parked, no one said anything for a minute.

"There is something so very wrong, Rudee my dear. I'm sorry I doubted you, because now I believe there is a plan, a conspiracy of some sort involving these strange characters who have been showing up lately at the club. They have tables on the balcony that they occupy every night. They pay no attention to the show, they only smoke and laugh their strange laughs and are rude to everyone. Tonight as I passed their tables, they were raising their glasses in a toast, and one said, 'The Sun King is dead. Lights out, Paris.' They all laughed loudly and clinked glasses as they would at a celebration. Rudee, what could this mean?"

"Sashay," he replied seriously, "did you hear about Les Invalides?"

She gave him a quizzical look, and he continued. "A symbol of the city that we love has been stolen — the cross from the Domed Church is gone and the dome has been painted black."

Sashay paled even more than usual as Rudee went on. "Mac, the domed church was built by Louis XIV, the 'Sun King,' and is one of the greatest monuments to a golden age." His tone grew sadder and a silence followed. "We must find out more. I saw Magritte, and the police don't take this seriously. They think it's vandals, and they're waiting for a handsome note or something."

"Ransom, Rudee, a ransom note." Sashay's voice sounded like it was coming out in little spurts. "Tomorrow night, they'll all be there. It's a party for the new owner." She didn't hide her disgust. "I can't get too close. They all stop talking when I come by and say rude things under their breath, and I think it's just a matter of time before they try to get rid of me anyway."

Rudee was shaking at this point, but before he could offer to defend Sashay's honour, I jumped in. "Let me go. You can get me in ... somehow. They wouldn't suspect me." Rudee was shaking his head back and forth so hard, his comb-over hair was trying to catch up.

"Your daddy would kill me, Mac, no-can-be."

Sashay was mulling over the idea, I could tell, and I knew that her opinion would win. I turned to her and tried to sound serious. "I'll listen and try to find out something about their plans, and that'll be it. Then we can go to Magritte with something concrete, okay?"

"She's right, Rudee," Sashay interjected calmly, "and I know how to get her in to the club. Come to my place, *ma cherie*, an hour before Rudee picks me up tomorrow night."

When she smiled at me, I knew that there was a special understanding between us. The danger seemed far away.

Nine

I was glad to be back on my curved wooden bed in my room in the Église Russe after all that had happened on my first day in Paris. I wondered if my class had seen the church before it was vandalized and hoped that Penelope was being inventive with her explanations for my absence, knowing I wasn't going to be rejoining them any time soon. I opened the hunk of a book I'd been looking at the night before, but it wasn't long before my eyes were swimming over pictures of beautiful old buildings, ancient churches with gleaming spires, golden domes, and crosses melting in the sun.

I thought someone with very bony fingers was rapping on my door the next morning, but as the cobwebs lifted from my brain, I realized it was rain on the dome above my room. It sounded like handful after handful of pebbles being tossed down on the roof as the wind wrapped around the windows with a comforting hush. Soon all comfort departed as my nose was attacked by the pungent odour of beets boiling below, beets with leeks or onions. Yech! My hunger was more powerful than my revulsion as I climbed down the stairs to Rudee's room. It occurred to me that he was trying to find a new way to drive me back to my classmates. Humming along to some intense organ music, he was contentedly stirring the awful concoction. I sniffed around for a morsel of bread or even some stinky cheese.

"*Bonjour*, Miss Mac," Rudee grinned, "hungry?" He read my expression and laughed. "Oh, don't fret. I know girls, and some women, don't like beets, especially for breakfast, but where I come from, it's the vegetable of kings."

Before I could ask where exactly that was, he closed his eyes and raised his head in happy concentration. "Listen, Mac, listen and savour genius. Vladimir Ughoman, the famous composer. Ahhh."

Then abruptly, he said, "Okay, let's go," as he snapped off his record player, grabbed his coat, and tossed me my duck's head umbrella. We raced through the downpour across the churchyard. "What do you say to a croissant and some fruit juice at CAFTA?"

The café was as busy as it had been the night before. Groups of cabbies were drinking out of steaming cups, checking their lottery tickets, and talking. I saw Blag arm-wrestling some helpless victim at a table near the kitchen.

"Hey Rudee, Mac," a voice called across the room, and Dizzy waved us over to a table he was sharing with another driver. After a round of backslapping and secret handshakes, Dizzy said, "Mac, I want you to meet Mink Maynard."

A small, dark-haired man with a furry beatnik beard greeted me with a sleepy smile and a low, rumbling voice. "*Mon plaisir,* m'dear, what brings you here?"

I glanced at Rudee. "My dad's a friend of Rudee's. I'm visiting from Upper Mandeville in California."

"*Très* cool, but I'm no fool," purred Mink, "you must be King Daddy's girl from halfway round the world."

Rudee and Dizzy laughed, and Dizzy explained, "Mink's the drummer in the Hacks. King Daddy's an old nickname for your dad. Mink also writes the lyrics for our songs." Turning to Mink, he added, "You don't have to prove it. We know you can rhyme."

"And keep time," Mink said to groans from his friends.

Breakfast arrived and filled the table, but it was soon just dishes and crumbs. Pushing back their chairs, Rudee and the boys did their secret handshake again, which by now was no secret to me.

"Practice Saturday? The usual?" said Rudee to nods from the others.

Dizzy nodded. "Ten-four.".

"And out the door," rhymed Mink as he headed for the exit.

Rudee said it was time for me to see a bit of Paris, even if it was raining. I persuaded him to drop me off at the student residence so I could check in and suggested we meet at the Pont Neuf taxi stand. This time the sidewalk was empty, so I waited until my group emerged with Penelope in the lead. She was wearing a Coco Chanel–inspired blue-and-white striped top and white capris, along with a severely pouty expression.

"Ah, *ma chère* Mac, we meet again."

"Penelope, I'm sorry. There's a lot going on. I'll have to tell you later."

"I assume this means you'd like to be excused from our visit to La Tour Eiffel, which will be followed by tea and macaroons at Ladurée," she responded petulantly.

I shrugged sheepishly.

"Okay," she said, assuming a take-charge tone, "take your shoe off and rub your ankle. Quickly, *s'il vous plait.*"

Mademoiselle Lesage swept into the street behind my classmates, who eyed me suspiciously. "Mac, Penelope told me about your parachuting accident in California."

"Oh, it's just a little flare-up, Mademoiselle Lesage. I'm sure with rest, it'll be fine."

"But today we are to climb the one thousand six hundred and sixty-five steps of the Eiffel Tower, just as Gustav Eiffel, its creator, did as he ascended to his office with its view of the exquisite Champs des Mars and the neoclassical Trocadero across the Seine...."

I got to my feet unsteadily. "I suppose I'll unfortunately have to miss today's activities."

Penelope mimed playing a violin behind Mademoiselle Lesage, and the others stifled giggles. I hobbled into the lobby and checked out the front page of *Le Devoir*, which featured a shot of the domed church surrounded by police cars.

In my spotless room with the bed still made, I quickly changed clothes, then headed for the Pont Neuf, grabbing baguettes and brie for Rudee and myself on the way.

We drove up the hill to Montmartre and sat on the steps of the Sacre Coeur church, looking over the magnificent city while an organ grinder pumped furiously on an ancient wooden box and a monkey dressed as a gendarme dashed through the crowd striking poses and collecting contributions in his little policeman's hat. Rudee dropped in a handful of change, then we headed down into the city.

"The financial section," said Rudee. "The wheelers and stealers," he added as we passed men and women in suits walking faster than anyone I'd seen yet in Paris. Caressing their portable phones like hand warmers, lugging shiny briefcases, eating hunks of gooey pastry as they walked, they seemed careful not to look at each other.

It was then that we noticed a big commotion at the Place St. Augustin. A jovial crowd was forming around a truck labelled "Fruits Fantastique" that had driven right into a sign painter's ladder. The driver and the painter were nose to nose. The driver was claiming that he hadn't seen the traffic light at all, never mind the colour. There were oranges, kiwis, and lichees covered in red paint rolling all over the square being squished by the cars trying to avoid the scene. The flics, as Rudee called the police, seemed to agree with the truck driver that the light was too hard to see and were preparing to let him go. This upset the sign painter so much that he climbed up the traffic pole and painted all three lights red as the crowd cheered him from below. When he climbed down, they carried him off on their shoulders to a bar down the street while the cars in the Place St. Augustin got more and more tangled. We sat on the hood of Rudee's cab and watched it all unfold.

"Rudee, that's the silliest thing I've ever seen," I said, laughing at the cars slipping and sliding, splashing fruit juice and red paint on the business people in their perfect suits.

Rudee nodded. "*Oui*, ridiculous, Mac, but to me it also is one more sign of something strange with the light in Paris. It's getting darker all the time." I saw what he meant. "I hope this traffic clears up soon. We've got to get you to Sashay's."

On the way we passed a tractor-trailer full of sand for a fake beach at the Tuileries Gardens pond, another "Lighten Up" project. A picture of a grinning Luc Fiat in his white suit filled the side of the truck.

"Hey, Rudee, look, a cup of California."

"*Excusez-moi*, Miss Mac?"

"Looks like Luc Fiat's been busy again," I said, pointing at the moving beach.

"We can use all the warm thoughts we can get right now, little one. It only shines on the sunny side of the street, you know," Rudee replied.

His odd expressions sometimes made it hard to respond, although I was starting to understand him better and kind of liked the Rudeeisms. Fiat's work, however, held a dark side for me. "Unless his bodyguards are keeping it from shining." I explained by telling him what I'd seen the day of the rally on the Champs Élysées.

"You're too suspicious," he laughed and handed me a tiny box wrapped in silver. "Give this to Sashay for me, will you? I'll be back in an hour, and I hope I will still recognize your little Yankee self."

He deposited me on the sidewalk outside Sashay's place and drove off.

Ten

I rang the bell at the side door and heard it echo from above. The door clicked open, so I started upstairs. The same foggy music that I'd heard in Rudee's cab oozed down the hallway on a fragrant cinnamon and lavender breeze. Sashay welcomed me to her "chambers," as she called her apartment, into a room that to me resembled a Christmas tree, without the tree. The room was lit by red candles. The light flickered off of a series of crystal ornaments hung at different lengths from a ceiling that was covered in waves of lacy white material that resembled frosting.

"Please be at home, little one," she said, indicating a velvet chair as she sat in its identical twin. It was my first real look at Sashay D'Or. She wore a serene expression with quietly intense eyes. Her face, with its beautiful and timeless porcelain features, was topped with a golden hairdo that had that whipped, baked, and glazed look of pure confection. A permanent pout suggested a "pooh pooh" to all in sight. She sighed as she spoke, and her narrow hands fanned and fussed through the lavender cloud around her.

"Rudee asked me to give this to you." I handed her the gift.

She took the tiny box with an even tinier smile and sighed. "Rudee, forever the same," as she opened it, revealing a pin in the shape of a silver peacock with its feathers about to unfold, hinting at the rainbow of colours to follow. "Ah, so elegant. He knew one of mine broke."

She paused and arched a painted lid at me. "You know about Rudee and me, I suppose." I nodded but wasn't sure I knew anything, really.

"It was … *l'amour* at first, as it always is; and then it just was, oh … *je ne sais quoi*." At this point I felt like I knew even less than before. "Rudee was, and still is, the most loyal man I know. He fought for me. He protected me and he made me crazy. Maybe I'm not meant for love."

Her voice trailed off, a mixture of regret and resignation, then she seemed struck by a powerful memory. Irritation crept into her tone.

"He smells of beets!" I tried to swallow a laugh by coughing, but I don't think it worked. "He sleeps with his gloves on, so the music never escapes his fingers, he says. This man stands on his head every morning. He claims it promotes hair growth. Has it worked? *Non*, of course not."

This time I couldn't disguise the laugh that escaped me. Sashay seemed to be gathering steam as she went on. "And the music, *mon dieu,* always the organ, always those mournful minor keys. And those melancholic composers — Gruntz, Langosteen, and worst of all, Vladimir Ughoman." Her lip curled beyond its usual pout as I recalled my own encounter with the *Churlish Concerto* that morning. One was definitely a full helping. She paused, sighed, and added quietly, "But Rudee loves me ... and I love him. It's just better for me if he's on the other side of Paris, you know. He calls me every day and tells me I'm the loveliest of all and that no one can dance like I can. Ah, maybe twenty years ago it was true, but now I get by on craftiness, some mysterious music, and the audience's desire to be entranced. What used to be all me is now mostly lighting, dry ice, and a three-drink minimum at work."

She stood up to pour some tea from a swan-shaped teapot.

"Sashay, I wish I could have seen you then," I said. "I'm sure Rudee's right."

Her smile made me feel like such a child. She slipped through a beaded curtain and returned with a long silver tube, from which she extracted a yellowed poster of a woman who looked part cloud, part whipped cream, her eyes glowing through all this motion and flashing like little jolts of amber lightning. The image of a young Sashay was magical, and underneath in ornate script was written:

Sashay D'Or. La Reine Des Rêves
The Queen of Dreams
One Show Nightly at the Lido De Paris

The same eyes looked at me as she rolled up the poster. "To work, we've both got a show tonight!"

From a gigantic shipping trunk, she pulled out miles of assorted fabrics and tossed them here and there. She draped me with each one then stood back, shaking her head, pouting, murmuring little "mmms" and "*ouis*" and "*nons*" as she worked.

"It's all scarf, Mademoiselle Mac, it has nothing to do with buttering your little cheeks with blush or balancing you on a pair of pumps with heels like La Tour Eiffel. It's not the scarf with the perfect little origami folds. And none of that awful whiplash look, wrapped around your neck like a maypole. *Mon dieu, non.*"

I agreed with everything, trying to stand still as she wrapped and unwrapped me in layers of satin, silk, cashmere, and chenille till I thought my neck would break out in hives. If my mom could see me now....

"And you don't want to look cold. One doesn't buy a watch for its ability to tell time, *oui*? We must drape, casually, elegantly, with that certain 'oh I don't really know how it fell like this' look. Once over each shoulder, a little toss to one side then the other. A little *pouffe* in the front, *et voila!* Oh yes, and let your hair fall in your eyes. It says 'so what.'"

I knew that part would be no problem. I can do "so what." Looking in the mirror, I felt silly but more ready for Le Moulin D'Or than I had been an hour ago. I was going to ask what to expect at the club when Sashay glanced through the curtains and spotted Rudee's taxi. "Our carriage is here, *ma petite*."

Eleven

As we zoomed to the club, Rudee kept glancing back in the mirror with, I thought, a mixture of amazement and amusement. Sashay swept me though the backstage door, down a dark hallway behind the stage, to her dressing room. From inside the club I could hear the blah-blah of voices and the occasional too-loud laugh, mixed with the sound of some old song that everyone but me remembers. As Sashay did a few salad-tossing moves with my hair, she whispered some last minute instructions.

"They'll be the ones on the balcony; you can't miss them. It's dark up there. Remember what Rudee said. Just listen and don't try to talk to them. You'll be subbing for Michelle the cigarette girl. If anyone asks, just say she's sick."

She must have read my expression as she looped a tray around my neck filled with every brand of cigarette on display. "Don't worry, you don't have to smoke to sell them. They'll order from you all night." Sashay kissed me on both cheeks and whispered, "*Bonne chance*. Meet me here after the show."

I turned to push my way through the heavy curtains beside the stage, and for a moment, my courage faltered. *What am I, a kid from Upper Mandeville, California, who isn't old enough to drive, never mind smoke, doing here? Will I fool anyone?* At that moment, the curtains parted and a small, elegantly-dressed waitress with a tray full of empty glasses almost knocked me over. "Oh, *excusez-moi*, go ahead, doll." She smiled and held the curtain open into the club.

My mouth went dry, and my heart skipped a few beats. The murmurs I had heard backstage swelled to a sea of voices, clinking glasses, and couples laughing, accompanied by a creaky piano player. The room was washed in cool green and blue light. It was filled with little circular tables, attended by waitresses bearing exotic drinks of every colour in every shape of glass. Lights in the floor resembled lily pads, and the ceiling seemed to have stars embedded in it. I was transfixed by the mood of the place; it was like nothing I'd ever seen. My reverie was broken by a voice that sounded like a cough. "Mademoiselle, while we're young, if you don't mind."

I followed the voice to a group of dimly lit tables set above and back from the main part of the club. I couldn't see the face behind the voice, but I heard the snide laughter that followed as I tried to steady my legs and start the climb to the balcony. My hair fell in my eyes, but I hung on to my tray and remembered Sashay's advice.

A single candle lit each table on the balcony, which was more like an alcove that overlooked the club. A group of five black coats and hats that I supposed had men in them were clustered around two of the three tables. The first thing that hit me through the dense cloud of smoke was the slightly swampy odour that hung in the air. That and the mirrored sunglasses. Two were wearing theirs; there were two pairs on the table, and the fifth had his hat pulled low enough to hide his features completely. "You want us to die of too much fresh air?" hissed the tallest of the group as the others laughed ugly, wheezing laughs. "What took you?"

Before I could answer, he grabbed a pack and some Moulin D'Or matches and tossed down a bill, waving me off like a mosquito. As I was about to make my escape, a bony hand grabbed my wrist. "Playing favourites, kid?" he almost whispered, then glancing at the selection, made his choice and looked me in the eyes. He had long, wispy silver hair beneath his hat and strangely smooth, bluish skin. A thin white scar snaked from his ear to the corner of his mouth. Minus the glasses, his eyes looked like what you see in the fireplace just before the fire goes out. I felt like my blood was slowing down in my veins from the cold chill that washed over me. "Where's Michelle?"

"Uh," I started to reply, but my tongue wouldn't move.

However, they soon lost interest in me, and I left as quickly as I could to gather myself. I was back and forth between the balcony and the friendlier patrons on the lower levels all night until the music stopped and the stage lights dimmed for Sashay's performance. I had turned toward the stage, excited to watch my new friend, when I heard a rasping voice from the balcony and saw a hand beckoning me back into the darkness. By now I was getting used to their cheesy comments and overall rudeness, but I was still on my guard as I made my way up the stairs. Suddenly I was pushed aside as a new group emerged onto the balcony from a doorway that I hadn't seen before. Two more cookie-cutter trench coats and fedora hats brushed past on either side of a small, slender man with slicked-back hair in a perfectly tailored suit and silver cowboy boots. The others greeted him like a celebrity, and I was completely ignored as I stood off to one side of their gathering. The little man eased around the tables shaking hands and saying, "Yesss, ouiii."

He stopped and addressed the group. "Kudos to the Shadows on Les Invalides. Dirty work and a clean job."

They laughed their sooty laughs as a tall, thin one held out a chair for him. "Congratulations to you, Louche. Your plan worked to perfection, and the cross is safely at Shadowcorps. The black paint was a stroke, ha-ha, of brilliance."

My body felt like it was frozen. I pulled Sashay's scarf closer to my neck and had trouble focusing on anything else that was said.

"You part of the *décor*, or are you working tonight, *bouffée*?" The little man at the centre of this thug party waved me over, to the group's general amusement. When he looked at me, I avoided his gaze, feeling like a specimen in biology class pinned to my place.

"Where's Michelle?"

"Sick," I mumbled, but it was my voice that sounded like it was on its last legs.

"What's your name? Where are you from? Not from here, I'm guessing," he hissed softly.

Mechanically I replied, "Mac. Upper Mandeville ... cigarettes?" I hoped to shift his attention to the tray that was shaking slightly in my hands. He ignored my question.

"Califorrrniaaa...." He stretched out the word like a lizard sunning itself on our backyard patio. "What do you think of the lighter, brighter Paris? Remind you of home?" he asked with a smirk as he opened a fresh pack of cigarillos and reached for a match.

My brilliant reply went something like, "Um, ah, yes. I don't know, I mean, yeah, I guess."

"Well, lighten up, kid," he sneered as he touched the match to the tip of his smoke, illuminating his face. I felt my arms go limp as I realized I was staring at Luc Fiat, the prefect of Paris. But how could that be? I was saved by a voice from below.

"Ladies and gentlemen, *mesdames et messieurs*, please give a warm welcome to '*La Reine Des Rêves*,' Paris's own Queen of Dreams, Sashay D'Or."

As the crowd applauded, I hurried downstairs and into the safety of the little space beside the stage to catch my breath. Sashay swept past me, and she seemed in a dream herself as strange music slowly wove its way through the club. Rhythmic blue lights like waves washed over the quieted crowd as Sashay, well, sashayed onto the stage, one long-gloved hand extended as if it were leading her somewhere. The music rose and fell. She seemed to pull endless wisps of gauzy material from the folds of her outfit as she spun and floated back and forth across the stage. Every once in a while, she would dramatically throw a jewelled, gloved hand into the air, and a little column of golden smoke would rise like it had been charmed out of the stage, while from somewhere a cymbal would crash in response.

Maybe it was the waves of blue lights, but I found myself feeling like I was beside the ocean in California, with the distant sound of children playing and my mom laughing at something my dad was saying. The sand felt warm on my hands and feet, and in the haze I could make out tiny sailboats in the distance as I watched the patterns the seagulls made on the sand as they drifted overhead. A particularly loud wave crashed, and it turned into the sound of the audience applauding. I realized I was still standing side-stage at the club. With a whiff of lavender, Sashay materialized and took my arm, leading me, in a fuzzy state of mind, to her dressing room.

"Mmm, I just had the coolest memories," I started to tell her. She smiled at me as she removed the cigarette tray.

"I know, I'd love to see the coast of California some day."

My head was still glowing from Sashay's performance as little questions started to take flight like seagulls from my memory. She seemed to know what I was thinking. "Later, *ma petite*, let's go. I don't want to see anyone at the stage door. I'll change at home, *chez moi*."

She threw a coat on my shoulders, and the next thing I knew we were in the back seat of Rudee's cab.

Twelve

The rain had stopped, but it had left the streets slick and shiny like new leather as the tires hissed down the grand boulevards. We didn't seem to be returning to Sashay's place in the Marais as we crossed the Pont Carrousel and drove through the archway past the Louvre. I sank back in the seat and listened vaguely to the usual exchange of jokes and recipes on Rudee's cab radio. The cafes and bars were still buzzing, and the lights on the beautiful Opera Garnier gave it a storybook glow. We continued on through a seedier part of the city toward the giant train station, Gare St. Lazare. We stopped at the end of a short bridge overlooking the rows of darkened railway tracks, and Rudee switched off the taxi lights.

"It doesn't look like much, but this is my first memory of Paris."

Sashay gave me an "I've heard this before" look as he continued mysteriously, "Everything old is in the eye of the dog."

I think Sashay coughed to hide a laugh, and we sat silently for a while. The night's events were coming back in a rush to me; the delicious fog that Sashay's show left had lifted. I tried to tell them everything I could recall about the "Shadows" and Louche, their leader. Rudee clenched his fists and gritted his teeth when I got to the part about Les Invalides.

"Snakethieves," he spat out.

When I reached the part about recognizing Luc Fiat, Rudee stopped me. "You must be mistaken, Mac; Fiat works for the mayor's office, and he is in charge of the campaign to polish up Paris."

I tried to tell him that I really *was* sure, but I had to admit that I hadn't been that close to Fiat on the day of the rally. When Sashay said, "It was very dark on the balcony, *non*?" I started to wonder myself what I had seen.

As Rudee switched on the headlights and eased back into the traffic, I asked about "Shadowcorps." He glanced at Sashay in the mirror and said, "That's the monstrous new building in Les Halles, isn't it? The ugly-as-snot light-reflecting one?"

She wasn't listening, instead looking out the window at the couples laughing arm in arm as they walked past the lights of the late night brasseries and bars.

Rudee caught my eye in the mirror and added, "I'd avoid that place like the flu, Mademoiselle Mac."

We dropped Sashay off outside the scarf museum and returned to Rudee's rooms at the Église Russe. "Hungry?" he asked, and without considering what that might bring, I said, "Yes, starving!"

He served himself a bowl of something pungent and steamy and made me a sandwich and a salad of something called *mâche*, which was better than it sounded, with cherry tomatoes. Had food ever tasted this good before? He chopped a pear and placed it between us.

"So, you see a career for yourself as a cigarette girl, Mac?" He grinned at my look of disgust as I recalled the scene at the club and sniffed my hair and clothing. "Well, at least as a detective." He seemed pleased with the evening's efforts. "But that's it for your little sniffer. I will call Magritte in the morning and let him know everything."

To me it felt like a jigsaw puzzle in which we'd found a few pieces that fit together, but even the frame was scattered in bits.

I climbed the steps to my room and fell onto my bed. Maybe it was the fact that my hair was over my face and smelled like an ashtray that woke me up some hours later, but I couldn't get back to sleep. I stared out the window at the now-quiet city and watched the light revolving around the Eiffel Tower, hoping it might lull me to sleep, but instead it was my thoughts that spun slowly. I pulled on my jacket. Maybe I'd just catch a little night air. Of course, I had a pretty good idea of where Les Halles was. I tiptoed past Rudee, snoring happily, his hands in his gloves resting on the blanket, keeping the music in.

Thirteen

The shops at Les Halles were long closed, but there were lots of stragglers on the streets in the area, some stumbling home from a long night of lifting glasses and emptying them, some looking for a quiet doorway to rest in until morning. This was a different Paris than the one I'd been shown so far, sadder and lonelier.

At night, with the lights out in the shops, the buildings looked the same, except for the old churches, dark and silent. I was about to give up, thinking what a crazy idea this was, wandering the city by myself at night, when a pair of truck headlights blinded me for a moment before turning down a narrow dead end street. If it hadn't been for the lights of the truck reflecting off its shiny surface, I would have missed seeing the building altogether. Then I saw the sign in raised letters above the steel doors: SHADOWCORPS.

The building was like a shadow itself, seeming to have no real shape in the darkened street, just a presence, and not a very pleasant one. The back of the truck opened, and two men got out and began unloading long, heavy-looking identical crates. The doors of Shadowcorps opened, and three more men emerged, one barking orders at the others as they assembled a conveyer belt that led into the building. I tucked myself into a doorway and watched them work with a mixture of curiosity and apprehension. As they finished emptying the truck, curiosity took over for the moment, and I inched down the wall beside the truck, hoping that they would be too busy and it would be too dark for them to notice me. Four of them struggled with the conveyer belt, trying to fold it up, and the one giving orders stepped away from the doors and snorted, "Can't do anything right without me, can you, you bunch of lugs?"

As they groaned and tugged, I saw my chance and slipped unnoticed into the foyer of Shadowcorps. A vacant reception desk provided the only hiding place. I told my breath to hold steady as the three men rolled their cargo on huge dollies around a corner and out of sight. I didn't dare look, but I heard elevator doors opening and closing and the sound of wheels and muffled voices, then nothing more. I waited for the silence to last a minute or so before quietly unfolding myself from behind the reception desk. My eyes slowly got used to the dark, cavernous lobby. It was completely empty — no plants, no directory, no signs telling you where to go, no chairs, no lamps, nothing. Even the reception desk was as naked as a landing strip. What kind of business went on here? And what was in those boxes?

My curiosity pulled me along to a set of elevator doors behind a wall that divided the entry area. The arrow above the gleaming silver doors pointed to minus five, and I stared at the dial, not understanding. With the exception of *G* for ground, all the floors were marked with a minus. The air seemed to blow around me like I was in a tunnel that went up and down, then it hit me — this building was completely and totally empty. I pushed the "down" button and waited, hoping that no one else was watching the arrow move at the same time as me.

I held my breath as the doors slid open, revealing what was more like a small room than a conventional elevator. I'm not sure what I would have done if someone had been there to greet me. I got in and pushed -5. The doors opened quietly onto a small hall. Nearby I could hear the sound of voices and activity and a lot of machinery in action. I peered around the corner into a vast warehouse-sized room with a low ceiling lit by tubes of bluish silver lights. Men in smocks, wearing goggles and holding blowtorches, were working on a piece of criss-crossed metal hundreds of feet long in sections of about thirty feet each. Was this what was being unloaded from the truck tonight?

At the far end of the room, a cluster of workers, also wearing goggles and heavy, padded gloves, were loading a giant hook into a huge fiery oven. I was so fascinated by this activity, I almost didn't hear the elevator doors hissing open behind me. I looked around frantically for a hiding place and had to take what I could find. I jumped behind a large rack on wheels, hung with cables, torches, and other tools that didn't look at all like the ones my grandfather kept in his garage. I crouched as low as my body would go. The crunch of three sets of footsteps stopped no more than a few feet from where I was hiding. Through the cables I could see only the bottom halves of their bodies, dressed in black, of course. It must be in season here. I spotted the shoes of the man in the middle of the little group. Actually, they weren't shoes at all, but highly polished silver cowboy boots, a sight that was becoming all too common for my liking.

"Did you remember to feed the gargoyles, Phlegm?" wheezed a familiar voice that I recognized as belonging to the bony-handed Shadow from the club.

"Yeah, bones and all, Scar," the other Shadow replied. "Looking good, Louche. Every construction crew in Paris would want to run this baby."

A third voice I'd heard at the table of ghosts added, in his own special hiss, "Except we'll be doing some deconstruction." If a snake could laugh, I think I knew then what it would sound like.

They moved closer to the work in progress, and I heard Louche, or Luc as I was sure he was, saying, "Yesss ... ouiii" approvingly as he examined what I now understood was a giant crane. He stepped up onto a workbench, steadied by a couple of his henchmen. The blowtorches were lowered, and the buzz of machinery slowed as he smiled and gestured at the proceedings. "Well done, my friends. The Shadows always work late, *n'est-ce pas?*" A ripple of quiet laughter reverberated in the huge room. "And in a few days, we will have our very own Bastille Day celebrations!"

My curiosity was disappearing, and my desire to be above ground was getting stronger by the second. I moved slowly along a darkened wall in the flickering bluish light toward a doorway that I hoped would get me out of there quickly. The workers applauded Fiat's words, providing the distraction I needed.

I stepped into an ancient passageway of large stones with puddles of blackish water pooling at my feet. One hallway led to another just like it, then another. Pipes twisted like ropes were attached to the walls, and the passages rose and dipped as I made my way through them to who knew where. The sounds of work became a dull throb in the distance. Even if I could find my way back, I knew it would be the wrong choice. That bad taste in the back of the throat called fear was making its way into my mouth. I was concentrating hard on not having it turn to panic when my shoulder bumped against a metal ladder. Feet dripping, I hauled myself up to the lowest rung and began climbing. I looked up into complete blackness, but it seemed to hold more hope than what was below.

After what must have been ten minutes of climbing, during which I did not slip once, nor think of how high I must have been, I saw light. I banged my head against something cold and hard and peered through metal bars onto a street. I realized I was looking through a sewer grate. Anyone larger would have been facing the return trip on the ladder, but not me. I tucked my hair into my hood and squeezed and pushed and wriggled until I was standing on a dark street, covered in things that should have been going down a drain, with wet feet and no idea where I was. A lone car sat at a taxi stand on the corner. I almost cried when I saw the exhaust pipes shaped like trombones. When I threw open the back door and fell in, I must have looked like a creature crawling out of a swamp.

Dizzy turned and looked at me from under his porkpie hat. "Where'll it be, *mademoiselle*? The Russian church?"

The street and the church were dark when Dizzy dropped me off back at Rudee's. He hadn't asked me a thing, and I don't think I would've had the energy to tell him anyway.

"The Hacks are rehearsing tomorrow. Maybe I'll see you there."

I thanked him and climbed past a snoring Rudee into the safety of my room. With my smoky hair and clothing smelling of the sewer, I was seriously beginning to compete with Rudee's stove for odour champion of Paris.

Fourteen

I woke with a start as rain rattled the windows of the turret. The wind cracked and snapped like sheets flapping in the storm, but I felt oddly comforted by the sound and fell back to sleep right away. I dreamed about surveying Paris from the sky sitting on a giant hook that swung gently in the wind, until I was dropped down a chimney that turned into an endless tunnel, out of which I landed hard on the ground.

"You alright, Mac?" Rudee called out. He must have heard me tumble from my bed.

"Yeah, I'm okay, Rudee," I answered groggily as I entered his room. He looked up a little sheepishly from burying his face in a bunch of flowers that he was putting in a tin can.

"From Sashay," he grinned, "to thank me for my little gift. She is the cream of the cat parade, no?"

Hard to disagree, I thought. I tried to wash last night off me in the tiny bathroom and thought about what to tell Rudee. I didn't have much of a chance, since he tapped on the door. "Hacks practice time. You coming?"

I didn't want to spend any time without friends, so I threw on some clothes and chased Rudee, who was carrying an armload of sheet music and a shopping bag to the cab. As he pulled out of the lane, he eyed me in the rear view mirror. "You slept late, *ma petite*. Storm keep you awake?"

I could tell he was checking out the bruised-looking circles under my eyes. I really wanted to tell him about last night's excursion to Les Halles and Shadowcorps, but he was acting so protective toward me that I felt guilty. He also seemed less morose than usual, even perky, as he chattered away like a magpie between rude gestures at anyone who risked sharing the road with us. "Last practice before the Bastille Day party." Mention of the national celebration made me shudder, thinking of last night. "What did you think of Sashay's dance, Mac? You know she is famous for taking the audience around the calendar to their childhood days when she performs. That's why they call her the 'Queen of Dreams.'"

I knew what he meant as I recalled my own reverie at the club.

"Bah, they won't let me in there. Not that Sashay wants me dangling around anyway. Blag's family owns the club, so I'm banned, and of course he can go whenever he wants."

Madeleine cut in on a burst of static. "*Bonjour,* all my low rollers, *ça va?* Just a reminder to all of you that the Bastille Day party at CAFTA features our very own Hacks starting after the fireworks ... if there's room on the stage for all that talent."

Rudee positively glowed at this announcement.

"Free blue, white, and red earplugs at the door!" Madeleine cackled, and it sounded like more static.

Rudee laughed and waved at the radio. "We'll show them. They'll be dancing their shoes away."

The practice was in a room above CAFTA that, as my dad would say, looked like a tornado had passed through it. Instruments, amplifiers, speakers, microphones, music stands, coffee cups, pastry wrappers, coats, and sheet music were scattered randomly. On the walls were posters of bands I'd never heard of like The Stereo Types, The Uncalled Four, and Colour Me CooCoo. I was sure I wasn't missing much.

"It's Mademoiselle Mac. She's back," said Mink Maynard from behind his drums.

Dizzy said "Hi" and gave me a knowing wink.

After a round of secret handshakes, Rudee introduced me to the brothers Maurice and Henri Rocquette on stand-up bass and banjo. They bowed and smiled, showing perfect teeth beneath tiny moustaches. Henri, the younger, had slicked-back grey hair, while Maurice, the older, had a shiny black dome that glistened like motor oil and featured a little hint of grey. Rudee handed out set lists and sheet music and from a shopping bag produced a collection of matching Hawaiian berets. "Part of the 'Lighten Up' campaign. What do you think?"

He tossed a beret to me, but I couldn't bring myself to try it on. Since there were no extra chairs, I curled up on a mound of coats and watched the Hacks storm through their repertoire. They seemed to forget I was there as the laughter got louder. They took turns playing solos, and the best ones were greeted with "bravos" from the others. The endings of the songs were ragged at first, sounding at times like someone dropping an armload of dishes. Gradually they got better as they went along, then they were on to the next tune, Mink coolly counting each song in by clicking his sticks together over his head and calling out, "One two, you know what to do." The song list included all their favourites, geared to keeping a party going, and there were a couple of heated moments while a sequence was arrived at.

"Nonono ... 'Grasse Matinee' can't follow 'Kiss My Sister.' They're in the same key!"

"Well, what about 'Gâteaux To Go,' then 'Stinkbomb Serenade?'"

"Are you crazy? They'll be throwing things at us." And so on.

It all culminated with an almost unrecognizable version of the French national anthem, "La Marseillaise," a very difficult song to disguise. My mind wandered as a long jam rambled on into the afternoon. Rudee and Dizzy were standing over me smiling when I came to as the others packed up their instruments. "I thought you California girls were partypoppers," said Rudee.

"Music for dreams ... so it seems," called Mink from behind his hi-hat.

"Nice to meet you, Henri, Maurice," I said.

"*Enchanté*," they replied as they headed for the stairs carrying their instruments.

"Hey, Rudee, let's grab a bite at Le Losange," said Dizzy. "I'm tired of the food at CAFTA, and we'll be seeing plenty of it at the party."

"Sounds good, Diz," said Rudee, who was polishing the chrome of his organ stand.

"Mac, you want to ride in style for a change?" asked Dizzy.

I looked at Rudee, who grinned. "Go bohemian, little one, you'll appreciate the higherlife after that."

As we walked toward the cab, Dizzy put his pork pie back on and tossed the Hawaiian beret into the trash. "Lighten up, *mon derriere*," he chortled.

The engine sputtered and coughed as he looked over at me. "Not that it's any of my business what you were up to in Les Halles in the middle of the night, Mac, but I figured we'd at least better have our stories straight. Rudee's my best friend, and he really cares about you. Since you arrived in Paris, he feels responsible for you."

I felt terrible knowing how last night's outing would affect my friend and protector. We wound our way up the hill to Montmartre. Dizzy pointed out an impossibly narrow brick building shaped like a lookout tower and identified it as Madeleine's office before stopping in front of the Sacre Coeur church.

"Dizzy, I know it was stupid, but I had to find out what I could. You know Paris is getting darker, not lighter, and I think I know who's behind it. Did Rudee tell you about what I overheard at the club?"

He nodded, and I went on to tell him the story of my late night visit to Shadowcorps. His eyes widened, and he pursed his lips. "Whew, this is serious stuff. Let's go. Rudee will be waiting; he has to know." I didn't like it, but I knew he was right.

Le Losange was a vaguely diamond-shaped brasserie on a busy corner. Rudee was already in a red vinyl booth by the window and waved us over. We all settled in and gave our orders to a waiter in a red apron that touched the tops of his shoes. He had an if-you-want-to-be-so-foolish tone as he noted our requests. I asked for ketchup on my green beans to see if smoke would come out of his ears, but he just ignored me.

I could only delay the inevitable for so long. Rudee told us through mouthfuls of oozing crêpe that he'd been to see Inspector Magritte about the domed church theft and told him about what I'd overheard at the Moulin D'Or. Apparently Magritte had a large map of Paris on his wall with pictures of the church from all angles, and a magnet of the missing cross that he moved around the map and some spaghetti-like scribbles.

"He took notes," Rudee related, "and seemed genuinely concerned. I could tell his hat was elsewhere, though, because he was distracted by a leak in the ceiling of his office that had just extinguished his pipe. When I left, he had opened his umbrella and was drawing more noodles on his map."

All of this just made me impatient, and with Dizzy's encouragement, I told Rudee about my visit to Shadowcorps. His expression went from surprise to shock to horror. "You climbed a ladder for five storeys and squeezed through a grate in the gutter in Les Halles?"

At this point his face was in his hands, and he seemed to be mumbling a prayer in some weird language. He looked up at me and put on his most serious expression. "Mac, I'm not going to go behind the back burner with you on this one."

I couldn't help it, and neither could Dizzy. We both erupted in laughter at once. Dizzy, unfortunately, had a mouthful of *tarte tatin* which wound up decorating the red vinyl beside Rudee.

"What?" Rudee asked indignantly, but I could see that he was trying not to smile. "Go ahead and laugh your heads till Thursday. I'm just glad Dizzy was at that cab stand."

A television set over the bar was showing pictures of the golden-topped monument in Place De La Bastille as we left the restaurant. It all seemed like preparation for the national holiday, until someone at the bar said in a shocked voice, "*Mon Dieu, non!*"

We stopped and turned in time to see the windblown reporter, mike in hand, breathlessly recounting the daring theft of the statue from the top of the column. She referred to "Another outlandish crime against the state and all that Parisians hold sacred. We ask not only 'why' was this beautiful work stolen, but 'how.'"

The camera pulled back to show the size of the square and the crush of cars swirling around it. In the background of the shot, I couldn't help but notice the ominous silhouette of a construction crane.

Fifteen

Rudee and I, with Dizzy following close behind, ran red lights from Montmartre to the Bastille. It came to me that the Bastille was today's major destination for my school group. I closed my eyes a lot on the way and was very glad when we joined a growing cluster of cars near the square. This time we were relative latecomers, since a crush of locals had gathered to stare at the now-naked column. The number of news trucks told us that this was going to receive much more notice than the previous thefts. A barrier was being set up, and the square was being taped off. Rudee charged past and ripped through the tape.

We spotted the bowler hat and tailored black coat of Inspector Magritte near a small group of official-looking men. "Rudee, *mademoiselle, monsieur*." He nodded solemnly as the three of us approached. "This is outrageous, of course."

"*Oui*, but Magritte, have you any idea who is responsible?" demanded Rudee.

At this point the inspector made a little steeple with his fingers, sucked in his breath, and narrowed his eyes in deep contemplation. "I have some suspicions and a couple of theories, but no clues and precious few leads. I'm considering every possibility."

Rudee looked like he couldn't decide whether to laugh or cry, but he asked the obvious question instead. "But how? How do you lift a statue from the Place de la Bastille and erase it with people all around?"

"Right now we can only say when, *mon ami*," answered Magritte as he nodded calmly and lit his pipe before continuing. "At a certain time every day in this part of the city, as the sun drops low on the boulevards, casting what I think of as a surreal glow over the city, the glare is such that it causes a few moments of blindness. Pedestrians stop and shield their eyes. It's why there are so many late afternoon accidents in the Place de la Bastille, you see."

I wanted to add that it might have something to do with the terrible drivers, but I didn't want Rudee and Dizzy to take it personally.

"If you will excuse me, I wish to consult with my technicians; they're dusting for fingerprints in the bistros surrounding the square."

As Magritte departed, Dizzy was already impersonating him, steepling his fingers and saying, "I'm considering every possibility."

Rudee was too disgusted to be amused. They were exchanging theories when I saw a small group of girls surrounding a woman waving her hands like she was fighting off a swarm of bees. Mademoiselle Lesage! I pushed through the group and put my arm over our sobbing tour guide's shoulders. She looked up long enough to register who was consoling her as Penelope fired off a half-dozen photos.

"Ah, Mac, I thought we'd lost you. I am so distraught. The golden figure represents the spirit of freedom, and the Bastille is the most sacred of historical locations in all of Paris because of its connection to the Revolution...." At this, she broke down and was unable to continue.

"Yes, Mademoiselle Lesage, I share your moment of misery, but we must soldier on in these trying times." Penelope gave a mock serious salute over Mademoiselle Lesage's shoulder. "Perhaps it would be best for us to return to the residence to contemplate in solitude this devastating loss."

Mme Lesage nodded sadly and half-heartedly gathered up the girls. Penelope came over and said quietly, "Well done, Mac. We'll probably head for Café de Flore in St. Germain once Lesage is safely out of sight. We used the fire escape last night. Any chance of you joining us for a *chocolate chaude*? The *clafouti* is *magnifique*. No almonds in sight."

"I'll definitely try," I replied, but Penelope wasn't buying it. "Look, if you can cover for me, I'll make it up to you, I promise."

"*D'accord*, 'Mystery Girl,' but this better be worth it, or you owe me a lifetime of tea parties, teen fashion shows, and pastry-making classes."

I nodded reluctantly. "Maybe we'll even play princesses like we used to," she added with a little too much enthusiasm. "Just kidding. Okay, get out of here before Lesage retires that handkerchief."

I eased back into the crowd, noticing lights and a TV camera, and made my way closer. I was stunned to see our favourite windblown reporter interviewing Luc Fiat. "But Monsieur Fiat, aren't these symbols of all that is light and right with Paris? How will this affect the mayor's campaign?"

He was slick, I had to give him that. With a little shrug and a patronizing smile, he oozed confidence. "You know, Louise ... and by the way, I love what you've done with your hair, it's so natural and windblown ... we Parisians are not so easily disheartened. The sun will come up tomorrow, hopefully, and we will carry on as we have always done. Yes, it's true, the loss of these beautiful golden symbols does take some of the glow from our hearts, but isn't that what electric lights are for?"

He chuckled greasily, and Louise seemed uncertain how to take this. Fiat went on, "But, *seriousement*, you know the smiles will be just as warm and the fireworks just as bright on Bastille Day, won't they? So, lighten up!"

She seemed glad to let the interview conclude naturally on this odd note and thanked him before returning to a recap of the crime for what was undoubtedly the hundredth time that evening.

Fiat stood with a frozen smile as she wrapped up. Suddenly his eyes caught mine when the camera lights switched off. "You ... *la petite* ... where do I know you from?"

I know I should've just smiled sweetly, and the moment would have passed, but I just couldn't. Instead I held his oily gaze and said, "Califorrrniiiaaa," before quickly slipping back into the crowd. Before I disappeared, I did see his perfectly waxed expression fail and change to something darker. I didn't want to stick around to see what came next. I heard Rudee calling my name over the hubbub of the crowd and the growing chorus of car horns, and we hurried to the cab.

"I have to take Sashay to the club. Do you want to come, or should I get Dizzy to take you back to the church?"

I said I'd rather go with him, and we said goodbye to Dizzy. Sashay was watching out of her window when we pulled up, and soon we were speeding toward St. Germain. They wouldn't listen to my repeated requests to assist Michelle, the cigarette girl, and I didn't mention my little confrontation with Luc or Louche at La Bastille. I had to beg to go in with Sashay and promise to stay behind the curtains while I was there.

I met Michelle. She thanked me for subbing for her and offered to pay me. I said no thanks, the experience was good enough for me. We chatted throughout the evening when she came backstage to refill her tray. It seemed that the Shadows were drinking and smoking even more than usual. Michelle thought they were celebrating something, maybe somebody's birthday. I had other suspicions but kept them to myself. The lights dimmed for Sashay's show, and the strange, hypnotic music began to seep into the club, along with the dry ice. I was finding a space where I could watch through the curtains when a voice whispered from the darkness, "Hey, *gamine*, you're blocking the way, move back here."

"Excuse me," I said, and was moving toward the voice that I thought must belong to the club manager when a pair of bony hands clamped my shoulders, lifting me up like I was weightless, and carried me quickly down a darkened hallway. I suppose I should have yelled or at least tried to kick my way free, but I was totally caught by surprise and I didn't want to destroy the mood at the start of Sashay's show. And yes, I was scared to death.

Sixteen

Before I had time to exhale, never mind scream, I found myself between two billowing black coats, being slid into the back seat of a long, low car with darkly tinted windows. The seat was soft and cushiony. In the back of my mind, I recognized this as the part in those black-and-white movies my parents love, where the private eye gets taken for a ride and warned to keep his nose out of somebody's business, or else, then he goes back to his office and completely ignores them. I waited for my warning from the bookends at my sides, but no one spoke, and not having anything to contribute, I sat in silence.

Out of the corner of my eye, I caught glimpses of them in the dull light of passing street lamps. They both had wispy silver hair and oddly unlined faces with that ghostly bluish tint to the skin. One was the scarred shadow with the bony hands, the other no doubt his pal Phlegm. The coal-coloured eyes staring straight ahead were cold and fixed. The steady streams of cigarette smoke and the little evergreen tree hanging from the mirror failed to disguise the slight rotting smell that clung to these two. I couldn't see the driver at all, just the shape of his shoulders and identical hat; he seemed to know where he was going. We moved smoothly along Boulevard St. Germain and across the Pont de la Concorde until we stopped just down the sidewalk from the giant "Roue De Paris" millennium Ferris wheel that lit up the square.

Once out of the car, they silently whisked me past a line-up that stretched in both directions from the ticket booths, right up to the platform where giddy Saturday night couples were piling into the waiting compartments. Someone entered from the other side of the car I was being led toward, and I climbed up and into the opposite seat as the doors were locked shut.

"There's no smoking in here, Monsieur Fiat." I attempted to reduce the tension for my own sake. He just stared at me until I wanted to take a shower.

"Yesss," he finally said, "you are a child, aren't you, after all." Our car jerked once, twice, as we started our climb. "What you know, my little flea, does not concern me. Paris is a city where things are easily forgotten. Old love affairs, people, places ... and sometimes that is as it should be."

He had a hazy expression as he looked over the city and down the length of the Champs Élysées. I flashed back to the rally where I had first seen him, and the moment seemed completely unreal.

"This used to be a beautiful city, you know, dark and beautiful. A city that respected its past. The little neighbourhoods, the narrow streets, the tiny houses huddled together; a place where you could discover passages that all but the rats had forgotten, lose yourself and hide your cares, not seeing the sun for days at a time."

This was all sounding chillingly claustrophobic to me, but he was just warming up, I could see. "Now, some fool builds a Ferris wheel to look down on the spot where Marie Antoinette lost her head."

He shot me a look that I think was designed to inspire terror. It worked. "One hundred and fifty years ago, the prefect of Paris, a man named Georges Haussmann, with the approval of that little worm Napoleon the Third, ripped this city apart. In a fever of demolition, they tore down all that held people's lives together and sold off the pieces to the highest bidder. Pushing these big boulevards from one side of Paris to the other, they ripped the soul out of the city in the process."

I wasn't even tempted to mention how cool it was that you could see the Arc de Triomphe from so far away. "Does your family matter to you, little one?" He stared into me. My mouth went dry, and I wanted to be able to give the right answer at this point. We had reached the top of the Ferris wheel, and our little car was swinging back and forth in the night sky. It was a long way down.

He went on without a reply from me. "My great-great-grandfather was a lamplighter at the time, and they snuffed out his job like extinguishing a lamp, tore down his family's home, and sold the pieces to scavengers who called themselves antique dealers. He died shortly after, selling postcards of the '*nouveau* Paris' to tourists in Montmartre. My great-great-grandmother whispered his story in my ear as a child at her one hundred and twentieth birthday party. I vowed to avenge him, and she died happily a few minutes later trying to blow out the candles on her cake."

I swallowed hard and clenched my teeth, pushing the picture of granny collapsing into the icing from my mind. A chilly breeze from the Seine blowing into my face helped me maintain my composure. Fiat continued his story as though I weren't there.

"I grew to hate the light of day. I collected sunglasses, carried an umbrella to school on sunny days. I was always happiest at the end of the day, when my papa would return home and entertain me with shadow puppets of buzzards on my bedroom wall. My best memories are of him waking me up and taking me into the street during power failures to see the 'true darkness,' as he called it, 'the shadow of the city as it once was.'"

Despite the bizarre nature of Fiat's story, I felt sad and nervous at the same time, wondering how all this was going to end. Our car jolted forward then backward, and La Roue de Paris started its spin. My stomach was beginning its own journey. Fiat's eyes bore into mine.

"History has its spin too, little girl. The new becomes the old and back again. Haussmann is ancient history, and all that he accomplished can be rubble if fate wishes it. A new vision of Paris is set to descend on this shiny place." Here, he took a pause that lasted too long for me. "And you won't get in the way of history, will you?"

I'm sure I was still shaking my head and whispering "No ... no" when the ride ended. Fiat evaporated into the night air, and I found myself being helped out of the car by a grinning attendant.

"A little dizzy, *mademoiselle*? Take your time down those steps. Thanks for riding with us tonight."

Seventeen

There's often a wind rushing across the Place de la Concorde; it's wide open and exposed. Exposed. That's how I felt, blown by that wind, not necessarily where I wanted to go. It was like all the happy couples waiting to get on the Roue de Paris were laughing at me. No doubt I looked a little green, confused, not sure which way I was going. I gave my head a good old California hair toss and tried to look purposeful as I walked to the nearest cabstand. Maybe I'd see a familiar face there, and I wouldn't have to hide my fear or confusion.

It seemed like a long wait. I'm not sure how long, but it was Saturday night, after all. I couldn't expect an instant rescue after the mess that, to be honest, I'd gotten myself into. I tried to erase Fiat's face from my mind, but it was replaced by Rudee's, and I had a pretty good idea of how unhappy he was going to be. Eventually, I worked my way to the front of the line and slid into the back of a dirty black sedan with cracked seats and some kind of frantic music playing. The driver, who was built like a small mountain range, turned his head and leered at me with a nasty smirk.

"Where to, nana?"

"Blag?" I asked, but there was no mistaking the driver.

"Actually, my name is Antoine. Blag's a nickname I got at school, and it wasn't my idea, but you don't get to choose those things."

I gulped, and too many thoughts came into my mind at once. Had he arranged to be here? Did he know where I had just been? I didn't ask, and I wasn't sure I wanted to know.

"This is rich," he snorted. "Daroo's been spitting beet juice out of his ears looking for you, and I get to bring back the prize. There's been a full taxi search for you, little Yankee twerp."

He couldn't contain his glee as he called in on his radio. "Madeleine, it's number 66; you can call off the hunt. I got the kid. I'll head for CAFTA now."

"*Oui*, Blag," came her answer. "Try to be pleasant to her. You can do it."

Blag grunted and turned up the bass on his radio to minor earthquake level. I noticed a collection of what looked like Viking action figures on his dashboard. "Listen to this. 'Clunque' by Malade. Now *this* is music. None of that lame nose-whistling stuff the Hacks play."

I wanted to jump to the Hacks' defence but thought better of it. I was also thinking about the welcome that awaited me at CAFTA.

"Uh, Blag ... I mean Antoine."

"What, nana, need to go to the *toilette*?" he laughed.

"No. So the cabbies have been looking for me?"

"Combing the streets is more like it, kid. The perfect chance for me to pick up some extra dough. Daroo's had his pantaloons in a twist since you disappeared from the club. What's the matter, Sashay's show too much for you?"

He suddenly accelerated and drove through a giant puddle at top speed, spraying a group of well-dressed diners coming out of a gleaming brasserie. He looked back at his handiwork in the mirror, waving a redheaded plastic Viking. I tried to hide my head in shame as he was gagging with amusement.

"Why are you so mean, Blag?" I didn't bother to correct myself this time. "And why do you hate Rudee so much?"

"Ruuudeee Darooo." He stretched out the words with obvious distaste. "I've been hearing that name since I was a kid. It's not even his real name. Ask him about it sometime, why don't you? You want to know why, I'll tell you. Our families arrived in Paris at the Gare St. Lazare on the same train, ready to start new lives in 'The City of Light.' We both came from nothing, but my family did something, and my father built the Moulin D'Or from the ground up, while Daroo's parents taught kids like us in the basement of the Église Russe. And just because he could play the organ, he was the golden boy; but when they needed someone to knock down a wall or move some giant piece of furniture, it was, 'Hey, Blag, give us a hand, will ya?'"

The resentment in his voice was heavy, and he paused before almost whispering, "I introduced him to Sashay. If we hadn't owned the club, she wouldn't have had anywhere to perform. Nobody buys that 'Queen of Dreams' act any more." He fell silent as we neared the lights of CAFTA. *But* he *still buys* it, I thought.

"Thanks for the ride ... Antoine." I tried to muster as much kindness in my voice as I could. I'd heard two tales of woe tonight, and I could've done without either of them. He just stared ahead, seeming to focus on the windshield wipers. I was glad he didn't come in with me to add to Rudee's stress level, and I needed a moment to collect my thoughts before heading inside.

As I walked into the bright light and warm oven smells of the café, the volume increased right away.

"Hey, it's the little runaway!"

"Rudee, your chick has returned to the nest."

"Hey, little one, is Blag your new best friend?"

Rudee threaded his way through the laughing and shouting tables of cabbies, trying to look amused, but I could read his expression from across the room. The ridge of his brow looked like a plow heading in my direction as he made his way to the door. I froze. I'd never seen Rudee like this. When he reached me, he threw his arms around me and squeezed me like he wanted to wring me out. "Little Mac, for flying out cloud!" His voice was trembling. "I was so worried about you. Where ... what ... oh, don't tell me now, let's go."

We rushed out the door to hooting from the drivers and into his car. As we drove to the church, the tension was awful, with Rudee shaking his head and muttering, "I was in a panic ... *mon dieu*...." as I sat very still and very small in the back seat. It kind of reminded me of that time I fell out of the tree and sprained my knee in my secret grove in the canyon, and my mom and dad and the neighbours had to search until they found me. They're happy you're alive, but once they get over that, you know you're going to hear the expression "just worried sick" a few thousand times before the night is over. Rudee jumped out of the cab and hurried down the path to the side door of the church, his hair flapping with every step.

I could see that the lights were on in his room, and I heard him saying, "Here she is, thank the clouds." Although I wondered who he was talking to, I was totally surprised to see Sashay sitting in Rudee's little kitchen. Her elegant swirl of scarves, skirts, and hair seemed so out of place in the bright little bare-bulb room with the lingering odour of overcooked vegetables. She swept me up in her lavender cloud and smiled calmly at me.

"This won't do," she whispered, and proceeded to light some candles, switch off the overhead bulb, and clear a space on the tiny table.

"Tea, Rudee?" She seemed to be offering, but it was Rudee who scurried about, lighting the kettle and digging through drawers for some prehistoric tea bag. I wondered how long it had been since Sashay had been at Rudee's place.

After the emotion and relief at seeing both of them again, I was ready to tell my story. There was no way to downplay what had happened to me, so I didn't really try. Sashay and Rudee listened intently, and I could read their reactions as I gave them the details — alarm at me being scooped up backstage at the club, anger at the Shadows driving away with me, and astonishment at my terrifying turn around La Roue de Paris. They pressed me for everything I could recall about the Shadows' car and their appearances. My revelation about the dark side of Luc Fiat seemed to surprise them, but I had the feeling they believed me. I wanted to talk about his twisted plans for the city and just what he might do, but these questions were pushed aside quickly by a wave of Rudee's hand.

"Little Mac, none of this matters. Your adventures have curtains now. I promise to take all of this to Magritte. It's time to get you back to your friends and home to your family trees." Rudee read my disappointment and tried to offer some consolation. "Don't worry, you have to come to the Bastille Day party. You must see the Hacks perform, of course, but then it's back to hundred-watt California for you, little one."

Sashay gave me a sympathetic look. "You know, Rudee's right. Nothing will happen to our beautiful city, and it's not worth taking any chances with you, *ma cherie*."

I knew that everything they said made sense. We drank our tea, and talk turned to the upcoming celebrations and plans. I found myself suddenly overcome with fatigue and just made it into my bed. I thanked the little wooden angels for looking out for me before tumbling into a deep sleep.

Eighteen

I woke to the loudest sound I'd ever heard. My turret room vibrated wildly, the windows shaking in their frames, the lamp dancing on the table. It took me a moment to realize that what I was hearing was music, but then I threw my clothes on and climbed down to Rudee's. A note on the kitchen table told me to follow the passageway at the top of the stairs and through the skinny door at the end. He'd added a *shh!*, but I could've screamed "Fire!" and someone standing beside me wouldn't have heard a thing.

I followed the note's instructions and, if possible, the music got even louder. As I opened the door at the end of the passage, the power of the wind alone made me hold on to the doorframe. I looked along the balcony of the Église Russe at the majestic gold pipes of the huge church organ. They gleamed blindingly in the Sunday morning light streaming through the stained glass windows. Behind the middle section of the organ, I saw hands flying above layers of keyboards then a familiar sight — the coil of Rudee's hair bouncing happily.

The music stopped abruptly, and I heard murmuring from below, first a single voice, then many voices chanting in unison. I looked over the balcony and saw that the early morning service was underway. Rudee caught my eye, grinned, and waved me over, indicating that I should keep my head down. I sat beside him on his bench as he whispered to me, pointing out the details of the enormous instrument he was in charge of. On the top of the middle section, perfect gold carved angels seemed to be dancing the shimmy. Rudee was obviously following the proceedings below, because at one point, he motioned me to one side and started to play something appropriately solemn. As the piece went along, he became more and more animated and ran his elbow the length of the keyboard in a mad flourish, shooting me a goofy grin. My shoulders started to shake, and I could feel the laughter escaping from my nose in little puffs. If only the congregation could appreciate this part of the service!

Rudee was in his element and started playing backwards, facing me with his hands behind his back. I started to lose control when he held one long, high, piercing note using his nose, and I knew I would have to escape. I crawled down the balcony and barely managed to get behind the passage door before exploding with laughter just as the music stopped. They must have heard me, I thought, and there was no way I was going back in for Rudee's next big number.

I quickly grabbed a crusty piece of bread (saving it from "death by beets") and some juice and decided to enjoy the day. Here I was in the most beautiful city in the world, so people said, and I felt like I hadn't stopped to look at it or really appreciate it. I knew that Sashay and Rudee were right. There was nothing I could do to change the fate of Paris. I might as well enjoy it before I had to go back to California, and I was going to have to account for my time to my parents. I still had some time to kill before meeting up with the tour at Notre Dame, the architectural wonder *du jour.* I was happily anticipating seeing the legendary cathedral, and I'd be glad if no one had tried removing or destroying part of it. I wandered over to the Parc Monceau, just around the corner from the Russian church, and entered through magnificent golden gates. It was filled with strollers, joggers, kids on blades and scooters, lovers kissing on benches under chestnut trees, and old folks sitting as still as the statues watching over the passing parade.

A light rain began to fall, so I opened my trusty duck's head umbrella, scaring a pigeon on the path beside me into a major flap. This amused me so much that I began opening my umbrella at every pigeon in sight, until I tired of the joke, well after the pigeons had, I'm sure. Gusts of wind lifted me slightly off the ground. For some reason, I remembered standing with Penelope at the bus stop one day when it started to rain. I guess she hadn't rinsed her hair too well, because bubbles started foaming on the top of her head until she looked as if she would float away. I was laughing so hard, I couldn't tell her what was so funny, and she just kept giving me that snotty look of hers until the bubbles began to fly all around her head and she finally figured out what was happening. Was I actually missing hanging out with Penelope?

I wandered without thinking about where I was going and found myself in a street market packed with people and food. A vendor's voice called out, "*Ohhh-ranges ... trois pour deux!*"

A little furball on a leash was sniffing for tidbits, which were plentiful under the stalls. Furball's owner teetered on high heels in full makeup and shades, long ruby nails picking over cherry tomatoes and radishes, baguette waving from a leopard print shoulder bag.

Trays of shrimp and crabs and clams looked like they had just washed up in front of the fish shop, while a giant swordfish presided over all, jagged jaw propped open. I moved on through a sea of faces and colours and smells — coffee, fresh bread, cheese, spices.

My rambling took me past the Place de la Concorde and the Roue de Paris Ferris wheel, which didn't seem so scary by day, into the beautiful Tuileries Gardens. The light rain continued on and off as I passed the old wooden carrousel and kids bouncing gleefully on the trampolines. A week ago, I would have been first in line for a good bounce, but today my heart wasn't in it. I wondered if I was, in some strange way, not a kid any more. I hadn't swallowed one raindrop today. I'd been admiring the reflections of the old buildings and shimmering trees in the puddles but hadn't even been tempted to jump into one.

As I wandered through the glorious gardens, the sky changed back and forth from black and blue clouds chasing each other across the sky to fistfuls of sunlight being hurled down upon the city. I realized that Paris was both a "city of light" and a dark and stormy place; it didn't have to be one thing or the other. At one point a cloudburst soaked everything while the sun continued to shine cheerfully, waiting for its chance to dry us all off again.

As I approached a circular pond with tiny sailboats scudding around in it, I saw another tacky emblem of the "Lighten Up" campaign. A fake beach had been constructed beside the pond with a row of beach chairs, each with a sun-shaped balloon attached. A wonky volleyball net sagged unused to one side, and instead of playing in the sand, the kids seemed to be happier kicking it into the water or at each other. A woeful looking character wearing a sandwich board that said MONSIEUR LE DUDE in glittery letters wasn't having much luck peddling sunscreen.

The craziness of this kept echoing in my head as I walked alongside the river, admiring the views that I'd seen in so many movies, books, and postcards

— the beautiful bridges and historic buildings and, of course, the glory of the Cathedral Notre Dame. Waiting for Mademoiselle Lesage and my classmates to arrive, I stood in awe of its ancient stones, the beautiful rose window, the incredible spire, and the wonderful flying buttresses that looked like praying mantis legs, holding up the walls of the cathedral. Spotting my classmates, I slid into the group a little guiltily, catching Penelope's usual expression of disapproval. While Mademoiselle Lesage regaled us with the rambling history of the building and its architectural details, Penelope told me that our guide had shown a whole new permissive side last night and had taken the girls to a jazz club in St. Germain called Le Bilbouquet, where, according to Mademoiselle Lesage, a combo that was *la bombe* had been playing. I, unfortunately, had apparently been too tired to join this expedition into the world of Paris nighttime cool. Just then something in our guide's portrait of Notre Dame caught my ear.

"... and although they were originally designed to divert water from the sides of buildings, these grotesque mythical creatures also came to be seen as images of evil. The gargoyles can take many forms — goats, monkeys, lions, and dogs ..."

A chill came over me and I heard Scar's words in my head: *Did you remember to feed the gargoyles?*

Instantly I knew there were some things I had to find out. I made yet another excuse to Penelope, seriously stretching the bonds of our friendship. She shrugged as if she was expecting this, and I eased out of Notre Dame and over the Pont Saint Louis toward the Marais and Sashay's place.

I approached the scarf museum and peered in the window. Busts of famous scarf wearers filled the small room, each wrapped stylishly in a swirl of silk or chiffon of different colours and patterns. A cravat section at the back featured dandies of the past with pencil-thin moustaches and berets. In the window, a bust that dominated them all featured a cascade of white material and a little plaque that read *Gift of Sashay D'Or, La Reine Des Rêves.* I smiled at the bust, which looked nothing like her to me, and decided to see if she was in. I rang, and her voice answered, distant and small. When I said it was me, she let me in right away.

The same red candles were burning and the familiar music played as Sashay led me into her apartment. It seemed to require an effort for her to smile at me, and there was a weariness about her that filled the room. She offered me tea and some powdery madeleine cookies and asked what I'd been doing today. I enthusiastically described my ramble around the city, but she wasn't really listening, just nodding in all the right places. I said I hoped I wasn't disturbing her or keeping her from something important, and a thin smile passed over her face. "No, little girl, I have nowhere to be, nothing to demand my time. I'm glad to see your happy face, because I'm afraid there isn't much happiness here today."

As she sighed deeply, I tried not to fidget, waiting to hear the story I was sure was coming, if I was patient enough. She fussed with the swan teapot, trimmed a couple of her candles, and looked out her window, almost forgetting I was there, it seemed. "I suppose I always knew one day I would have to fold up my scarves and put them into the trunk for the last time."

Her shoulders sagged under the weight of her latest sigh, and I was beginning to feel deflated myself. She looked at me from under her waxy lashes. "I suppose you would not know that tomorrow is my last night at the club. They're closing it for renovations then reopening it as the Moulin Noir. I don't fit the new look of the club, and I doubt I would want to, from what I've heard."

Rumours of an "Underground" theme were circulating, with stacks of fake bones and a cave-like feeling to the architecture. "Rudee tells me that he'll help me find another place to dance, but I don't think he realizes how impossible that would be. People don't want the same things when they go out now. Everything has to be loud and blindingly bright, so you can't hear or think or feel anything at all."

I told her that we have places in America like that. They're called malls.

She smiled and said, "Last night was my first time at Rudee's apartment in almost ten years." Her nose curled a bit in recollection. "The time before that, he had broken his leg falling off the church organ; that's still something of a mystery to me."

It was my turn to smile as I recalled this morning's spectacle. "Sashay?" I started slowly. "There's something I've been curious about."

That knowing look came over her serene face. "How does your dance work? I mean, how do you make people feel like I did, like I was a young kid on the beach again?"

Sashay nodded, and I had the sense that she was considering how much she could explain. She refilled our teacups and seemed to be looking at something that wasn't there. "I guess I have my mother to thank for most of who I am. She came to France with a family of gypsies, part of a religious group called the Dervishes. They danced a special swirling dance together that sent all who took part into a kind of trance." She looked at me to see how this was being received. I was fascinated.

"My father belonged to a new group of mystic French magicians, and two people like my parents were probably destined to meet. My mother taught me the ancient dance of the scarves and how it takes people back to places they've loved." Here she paused and arched a painted brow before continuing. "My father showed me how the perfect scent, the mood of the lighting, and the mystery of the music helped prepare the audience to be taken away from the everyday world." Sashay allowed a quiet calm to pass between us before adding in a happier tone, "Maybe I will show you the dance sometime. Would you be interested, *ma cherie*? I have no one to give this to. And you look very good wrapped in the scarves!"

We both laughed, and I realized how good it was being with Sashay. I felt like I could tell her anything. I took a deep breath and told her that I thought Fiat and his gang were going to do something terrible, very soon. I didn't know what it was, but if they could steal monuments and maybe make Paris darker by the day, it could be pretty bad. I just didn't believe that the police, if Magritte was any example, had a chance of preventing anything from happening. Not that I did, by myself, but if I could find out something definite, well maybe somebody powerful could prevent them, somehow. I told her that I wanted to go back underground to where the Shadows did their dirty work and take a look. Could she get me there, I wondered?

"Ah, Mac, even if I could, I'm not sure this would be a good idea. But I see that you're serious about this. I have a thought. Do you remember Jerome, the *bouquiniste* you met when you first arrived?" I nodded and smiled when I thought of that bushy face and my first impressions of Paris. "Let's go and pay him a visit, shall we?"

Nineteen

Sashay had a different set of scarves for the outside world, but the look was still all hers. She wrapped me in one the colour of the inky clouds that had been passing overhead all day, and we started walking through the Marais. The narrow streets were filled with couples, families, and tourists, sitting in cafes, wandering in and out of the shops, all at a slow Sunday pace. After crossing three small bridges in succession and passing over the tip of Isle St. Louis, we walked past the rows of *bouquinistes* lining the river. Smiles of recognition were exchanged between Sashay and many of the vendors, but we didn't pause to browse the books or pass the time of day. As we came to the last set of stalls near the Pont Neuf, I recognized Jerome, deep in conversation with a couple of customers over some dusty book of black-and-white photographs. He caught Sashay's eye and wrapped up the book for its new owners.

"Madame D'Or. What a pleasant surprise."

They exchanged a whirlwind series of little air kisses. When it was just the three of us, she leaned in close to Jerome's bearded face and whispered a few things that I couldn't hear. He nodded seriously and looked back and forth between her and me. "For you, Sashay, of course. We river rats know all the ins and outs around here, don't we?" He turned to me. "So, life above ground not exciting enough for you, little one?"

I shrugged and smiled, not sure how much she had told him about my mission. "There is a way that I know, but it's very difficult to get in." He looked me over and added, "You might be just small enough to fit through a sewer grate, but it would be quite uncomfortable, you know."

I didn't bother saying that I had a pretty good idea of just how uncomfortable it was. I just continued smiling. "I'll close up early and take you there myself. It's best that way. Always good to see you, *ma reine*."

Another flurry of cheek pecking took place, and Sashay leaned close to me. "I'll cover for you with Rudee, but please be careful. I could never forgive myself if ... this scarf, by the way, could be helpful if you wish not to be seen."

She hugged me and swished away as only Sashay can. I watched people watching her as she passed. Jerome finished bolting down his book stall and said,

"*Allons-y*, let's go, *ma petite*. It's a bit of a walk."

We took the steps down from the Quai so that we were walking right alongside the river. As they waved and shouted greetings, it occurred to me that Jerome knew a whole other type of Parisian than I had met so far. He spoke to sun-cracked men and women on boats, coiling ropes or washing down decks, crusty toothless card players at wobbly tables with a label-less bottle in the middle being passed around as play went on, and assorted other "river rats," as he called them. He was the perfect tour guide, mixing in bits of history of the Seine with colourful stories of life by the river. He also told me about the supposed underground Paris.

"I've never seen it myself, but I'm certain that it exists. These people you call the Shadows are no doubt the ones who were born in the tunnels under Paris and have lived their whole lives there. It's said their eyes are so sensitive that they can never be exposed to natural light without being temporarily blinded, and that their skin is unnaturally young for their whole lives. But I don't know any of these things for certain."

It sounded like a pretty good description of the characters I'd encountered at the club. We stopped under one of the bridges. I wasn't sure which one, because we'd been walking and talking for a while. Jerome gestured toward a grate in the wall. *No problem*, I thought. Compared to my last sewer experience, this was like the doors of a department store.

"I don't know why you'd want to be looking underground when you've got all of Paris to explore, but that's up to you," he said.

He put his hand on my shoulder and added seriously, "Watch yourself, now. I don't think these Shadow types are your kind of people. And if you get in trouble, look for one of the river rats. They'll always help someone out if they can. I guess you won't be needing this tonight. Would you like me to take care of it for you?"

He smiled and indicated the duck's head umbrella. I laughed and handed it to him. "Thanks, Jerome. I'm sure everything will be fine."

As he made his way back along the riverside, I waved and hoped it was true.

Twenty

Of course, it was more of a squeeze than I'd thought, but I soon found myself on the top rung of a ladder with a deep darkness rising from below. I took a couple of breaths and got settled, not knowing what awaited me at the end of my climb down toward a rumble of indistinct voices and activity. After about five minutes of descent, I could make out the cold stone surface that the ladder was attached to and sensed that I was close to the sounds that were echoing upwards. As I peered past my feet, the darkness seemed to be changing shape. Swirls of light moved like cream floating on a cup of coffee. The blackness gave way to shades of grey, and buildings emerged from the stones below. I fought off nausea as the stench of the sewer rose to meet me. I stopped for a breath and leaned back as far as I dared, looking over one shoulder then the other. The rumble was the sound of human activity.

What lay below me was the underground city that Jerome had spoken of. I realized I was climbing down a wall between two buildings that looked out onto a sort of street. I say "sort of" because it wound snake-like with passages shooting off in odd directions. The light was the same harsh metallic blue that I'd seen in the workshop on my last trip underground, and it began to illuminate the world below. What at first resembled wisps of smoke became people passing each other. Long, thin vehicles like tiny Métro trains without tracks rumbled and rolled by. Piles of rubble were scattered around, and drilling was going on in a couple of places I couldn't see. Buildings had been carved roughly out of the stones, and the light that slipped through the cracks suggested a cave dwelling type of existence. Who would live here? What went on in a place like this? Did they eat mushrooms for breakfast? I'd soon find out.

As I touched down, I was grateful that my climb was over. I'm not afraid of heights, but you can only spend so much time suspended above the ground without some unease. The sense of relief passed quickly as I realized I had no plan, no clue where I was, and no one to help me figure it out. In a place of permanent midnight, you can't wait for dark, so I took a deep breath and moved slowly toward the street. Strange people passed each other without speaking or even noticing each other's existence, but I'd seen that above ground, so it didn't seem so odd.

A clattering sound of wheels on stone warned me of an approaching mini Métro train, and I ducked behind a convenient pile of smashed-up rocks to watch it go by. The windows were tinted to make visibility impossible. A band of light where you might expect a bumper seemed to guide it down the stony street. Exploring as best I could without being noticed, I looked in slits of windows to observe the workings of this weird place. I was starting to get oriented and found I could fairly easily slip from one hiding place to another. I had no idea what anyone would do if they saw me, but I didn't want to chance it. Certain passages were quieter and had odd-shaped doors with numbers that suggested homes to me. The streets the trains went through were a little wider, noisier, and there was more activity inside and out of the buildings. Curious as I was to see a Shadow shop, it wasn't the time or place for souvenir hunting. A siren sounded and a horn blasted repeatedly until a mechanical voice came over a loudspeaker.

"Three point five slide in P 27. Crews blue four and five to P 27. All others avoid area."

Within seconds, two groups of helmeted Shadows with shovels, picks, metal wagons, and dull blue flashlights zoomed past and out of sight. My heart resumed beating. I was tucked in a doorway waiting for the commotion to end when two figures approached, one looking very familiar. Beside a standard issue Shadow shape was a beefy hunk of human with more meat on him than a six-pack of Shadows. Blag! What was he doing here? I caught a snatch of conversation as they passed within inches of me.

"... how do you live like this? Everything falling down around you. Man, I'm no neat freak, but the stench down here could peel paint. What, no cleanser, smokey?"

I guess I shouldn't have been shocked to see Blag with one of the Shadows, but it still took me by surprise. I'd kind of felt a bit sorry for him the other night when he'd picked me up and taken me back to CAFTA. Now I felt disgust, or worse. A chillingly familiar voice answered him.

"It wasn't always like this, big boy, but it's getting worse. Four or five slides a day, some bad. Last week a whole passage was blocked and abandoned. But Louche has a plan. Fear not, squarehead."

It was the voice of Scar, the bony-handed Shadow from the club. They turned a corner and I followed, slipping in and out of doorways and spaces between buildings. The streets got quieter and the passages narrower, and they walked in single file until reaching a polished metal door recessed in a rock face that could easily have gone unnoticed. They stopped, and while Blag looked around and kicked at some loose stones on the path, Scar hissed the words "Black Mamba" into the door, and it slid open to admit them. For one terrifying moment I thought Blag looked right at me as I leaned out a little to see what they were doing, but then he turned away and passed through the doorway.

I seemed to be alone. The sounds of activity were in the distance, and even the ever-present sewer reek had faded a bit. I approached the shiny steel entrance to who-knew-where and stared at it. Sealed air-tight like a bank vault, it was perfectly smooth, with no doorknob or window to mar its gleaming surface. There was a small button on one side mounted with a speaker in the rock, and I knew what I had to do. I pushed it, and when a red light went on, I forced my voice as low as possible and barely whispered "Black Mamba." The door slid open silently, and I stepped inside, grinning.

What I saw couldn't have been more different from the stinking underground city just beyond the entrance. All was smooth and metallic instead of rough and rocky. Was that a faint odour of mint? It could have been ether; there was a somewhat chilly, hospital-like feeling to the place. I could see what looked like a satanic supermodel working at a computer in a waiting area. She was dressed in designer black leather and stiletto heels that looked like they could be used for acupuncture. Her hair was pulled straight back from her carved features, and her eyebrows resembled French accent marks. While she concentrated on her screen, I slipped past as quickly as possible, blocked from her sight by a huge vase of black roses. The sleek hallway was covered with black-and-white photos of every possible phase of the moon. Deep carpeting added to the funereal hush of the place. Expensive, tasteful, and slightly terrifying was the mood *du jour*. Passing offices with the doors shut and the throbbing glow of computer screens inside, I wandered for some time without seeing anyone until I turned a corner and almost walked into a pack of Shadows, all lighting up together. They sucked up the smoke like nutrition, and when they exhaled, it was a wonder they could see each other, never mind spot me.

"Okay, it's time," muttered one, and they all seeped into the nearest set of doors.

I followed at a distance down a stark blue-lit hallway as they joined others gathering in what looked like a science fiction laboratory, a room full of gleaming tubes, keyboards, and screens displaying charts and strange symbols. Dominating it all was a huge fish tank–like structure holding what appeared to be floating, spinning, sparkling drops of water, dancing like fireflies in the glassed-in space. A chubby scientist type, who looked like a Shadow in reverse with jet black rock star hair and a silver flowing lab coat, paced, hovered, and made adjustments as the group settled around a table. While the smoke and reek of this lot was disgusting enough, it made it easier to remain unnoticed in the hall. It was no surprise to me when the master of nasty ceremonies eased in through a side door and shook hands with the rock 'n' roll doctor. The general coughing and clearing of raspy throats subsided as Fiat took command of the room.

"*Mes amis*, sons of the darkness ... ouiiiii ... yessss. The hour approaches when Paris will belong to the Shadows once more. When we will never again have to crawl back into the cracks, ashamed of what we are."

I noticed he said "what," not "who." Low coughing sounds of agreement rumbled through the room. He went on, "As the lights of the city have dimmed, so too will the hearts of all who cannot embrace the darkness. As you know, our plan calls for 'lights out' during the Bastille Day fireworks, when the city will have other preoccupations, but that is just the beginning. I would like to introduce you to a friend of the underground, the brilliant Dr. Etienne Brouillard."

More mucousy coughing and laughter like the hissing of leaking pipes greeted this announcement. The doctor, looking a bit sweaty and trying to appear dignified after this introduction, had the lights dimmed for his moment of glory and belched into his hand. I felt like I should be passing a "teacher is a pig" note to Penelope at this point.

"What you see in this tank," he gestured to the glowing, floating specks behind him, "are clouds. Very small, almost invisible, but clouds indeed. And very smart clouds, because they have been individually charged to be self-sustaining once released. They devour dark matter — cigarette smoke, automobile pollution, industrial fumes, political conversation...." at this point, he allowed himself a swinish smile, "and they grow and hover over the city, keeping it in a never-ending midnight."

The doctor looked very self-satisfied as bits of spittle formed at the corners of his mouth. He began speaking more rapidly. "We have seen how they have slowly darkened the city in recent weeks.

At a signal from Monsieur Fiat, millions of them will be released through the sewer grates all over Paris." He snorted audibly at this point, and his voice grew louder and higher pitched. "The clouds will cast a shadow over the city, a beautiful shadow that will never pass, one that ..."

Fiat signalled to turn the lights up, cutting off the foaming doctor and starting a brief burst of applause from the Shadows, who seemed more than a little confused by this demonstration. "*Merci*, Monsieur le Docteur, *merccci*. Yesss, but before that happens, there is one symbolic act that will cast the heart of Paris into sweet despair. The giant crane you have been working on so hard is finished, my friends, and tonight it will be wheeled into position beside the Seine in the Square Jean XXIII, where it will appear ready to go to work like so many others the next morning — fixing, building, repairing ... but it has a different destiny, does it not?"

Here he paused dramatically as the Shadows nodded and grinned their snaky smiles, knowing, no doubt, what was coming next. "And as it readies to pluck the spire of Notre Dame like a spiky blossom from the cathedral, I will personally inaugurate the launching of the great darkness ... with this."

He held up what appeared to be an expensive, oversized bottle of champagne filled with black liquid. "Good enough to destroy the golden shine of the dome of Les Invalides, good enough for the rose window of Notre Dame, *non, mes amis*?"

As he called out a final "All right, let's go ... much to do," over the swell of approving sounds in the room, the meeting broke up into little groups that began to disperse. I slipped into a closet to hide until all was silent. I couldn't resist taking a closer look at the cloud tank as I passed quietly out of the room. The sounds of Dr. Brouillard chewing and grunting from an adjoining room covered my departure nicely. Up close, the tiny clouds looked like pinpoints of liquid light, glowing from within, all whizzing around the tank like they were dying to escape and do their worst. At least that's how I imagined it. Back in the hallway, I took a long breath and figured it was time to get out while I could. I had more than I needed to go to the police with. How to get out of here?

At that instant, heavy footsteps pounded down the hall toward me. I jumped back into the lab just in time to watch Blag crashing down the hall with a ferocious scowl on his face, no doubt sent on some nasty mission by Luc Fiat. After a bit of time had passed, it was quiet once more, and I thought I'd head in Blag's direction. Instead of exiting, though, I found myself in a circular space with twin elevators painted to resemble the Arc de Triomphe at night with hallways fanning off like the boulevards at L'Etoile. Clever, but bizarre. Cool blue light oozed from above, and looking up, I saw one large room or office encircling the area with partially opaque glass. A strange scene was being acted out on this circular stage. Two identical figures gestured at each other in silhouette like a mirror with a delayed reflection. One would step forward, raising his arms and dramatically dropping them to his sides, then the other would respond with almost the same moves in reverse.

I watched, fascinated and intensely curious, until I saw one of the figures lift something large and pointed over his head and swing it wildly at the other. He must have missed his target, because the glass above me suddenly shattered with a huge crash, and jagged pieces flew into the air. I dove into the nearest hallway and watched while a vast panel of window opened to reveal Fiat, trembling and holding a shining golden cross at his side.

He spat out his words at the figure across the room. "I should've known when you told me to "Lighten up, Louche" that your ridiculous campaign was no cover-up at all. When we were children, you always put the sun in your pictures, didn't you? And you were terrified of Papa's shadow buzzards while I loved them. And don't think I didn't know about your secret weekend tennis and volleyball; that make-up didn't hide your tan, you little lizard."

I couldn't hear the reply from the other side of the room, but I was furiously trying to figure out what all this could mean. The menacing voice lowered to its usual serpentine hiss. "Go ahead. You've served your purpose well, confusing people who can't tell us apart, but now I don't need you. It's too late to stop me anyway, and you, of all people know it. Soon enough the Shadows will emerge from the underground, and I'll be the king of midnight, rolling through the blackened streets of Paris in a limousine as long as a city block with a golden cross for a hood ornament."

He stood glaring as he tossed the shiny weapon to one side. At this moment the elevator door opened, and out strode ... Luc Fiat!

In a rush it all became clear to me as he swept down one of the corridors looking like he was in a trance. In the office above, Louche, his twin brother I now realized, picked up his phone. "Phlegm?" He sounded completely calm. "My brother just left my office. Unfortunately, he'll need to be detained until after the celebrations. Make him comfortable in *suite zero, s'il vous plaît*."

As I craned my head up to hear what Louche was saying, at that moment he decided to inspect the damage to his office window and looked right down into my eyes. A twisted smile came over his face.

"Ahhh, *ma petite. Bienvenue.* How perfect. Welcome to the underworld."

I was frozen in place and helplessly watched him pick up his phone again without taking his eyes off of me. "Scar. We have an intruder in the Shadowcorps offices. A little puff of nothing. Ouiiii, good idea. Bring the gargoyles."

He hung up, and a smile like the gleaming blade of a knife hung in the air until I ran and ran.

Twenty-One

Hallways led to more hallways and a blur of doors and voices and the sound of my breath racing in and out of me. Each time the voices got closer, I'd make another turn, but I knew I couldn't keep it up. Finally, I recognized some things — the photos of the moon, that giant vase of black roses. It was the entryway, and there was the zombie supermodel receptionist. As I was trying to figure out how to get out unnoticed, the doors opened, and the hushed entryway was suddenly filled with a pack of the nastiest-looking creatures I'd ever seen, growling ferociously and pulling on the metal chains that were held, just barely, by Scar. Their skin was stretched like shrink-wrap over their bones, their eyes seemed lidless, the fangs were permanently bared, and their ears flat back against their knobby heads. It was a terrifying sight, and I struggled to keep from gasping behind a couch, my latest hiding place.

"Oh, Scar, you look so manly with your puppies," sneered the receptionist, arching a razor-sharp brow.

"Let's cut to the chase, if you know what I mean, Tawdry."

"Your little pack of underdogs seems a bit more restless than usual," she offered teasingly.

"Must be that perfume of yours. What is it — eau de toilette, or oh, the toilet?" he wheezed and laughed in his ugly way.

She raised a brow in the direction of the hallway to the right of her desk, and Scar rushed on, led by his straining beasts. He was no sooner gone than Tawdry whispered, "Okay, little one, you can come out. I'll open the doors for you. I'm outta this dump soon enough myself."

I emerged wide-eyed, and she shrugged, flashing a little so-what smile. She indicated a row of security cameras on her desk, one clearly showing the outside of the door. "Can I hear that voice again? You know, 'Black Mamba'?" She smiled and imitated my entrance trick. "Okay, quick. See you in the sunshine, kiddo."

I didn't even stop to thank her as I burst out the sliding door and down the nearest stone passageway. The stench of the sewer was never so welcome. I could hardly wait for the sweet smell of boiling beets. After a while I felt like I'd traded one maze for another. I passed piles of bones in little alcoves and had to dodge the stalactites that were hanging like rocky icicles from above. At times the water got deeper, blacker, and nastier smelling. The light was virtually non-existent when I almost ran right into a wall of stone. A rockslide! This meant I'd have to turn back. Right then I heard a sound that stopped the breath in my chest. My stomach rose into my throat, and I felt pure cold fear. That snapping, snarling sound could only be one thing. The gargoyles. A voice hissed, "They're pulling this way. C'mon."

I started groping a wall looking for a crack to crawl into I knew didn't exist. Suddenly, from above, a huge hand reached down and grabbed me by my coat while its partner clamped over my mouth just in time to stop the scream that was about to escape.

In the darkness, I could see nothing. The panting and slobbering of the gargoyles seemed to fill the space below me. A gruff voice barely whispered in my ear, "Be cool and very slowly take off that scarf, and we might get out of here."

Blag, my rescuer? It didn't make sense, but this wasn't the moment for making sense. I slipped off Sashay's scarf, and he indicated that I should wrap it around us. He continued to support me with a grip of steel that I was very grateful for. His other arm was coiled around the jagged point of a rock at the top of the slide. The scarf blended in with the rocks and must have concealed us, because I could feel the hot hound breath and see flashlights moving over us.

"She must be close. These gargoyles are goin' crazy," a voice grunted.

"Yeah, right, she turned to stone," came the snide response.

"Alright, alright, let's keep looking. Louche doesn't like to wait."

The sound of chains clanking together was accompanied by growls and yelps. Gradually the sound receded. I was still afraid to breathe. My leg was going to sleep, and I shifted slightly. A sudden torrent of tiny stones rushed down the rock face.

"What was that?" a distant voice echoed down the passageway. Some whining and snapping followed.

"Let's get outta here before this one closes off."

Great. Something else to worry about. Hungry creatures with fangs like sharks, a madman who wants to plunge a beautiful city into darkness, being wedged in a stinking hiding place with a sweating lug who might or might not want to protect me, and now the possibility of a rock slide trapping me in the Paris underground forever. Whatever happened to just worrying about too much math homework?

Once the silence took over, Blag groaned and eased me to the ground. I realized he'd been holding both of us up with one arm for quite a while by hanging on to a large chunk of freshly broken rock. "Thanks. How, how did you ... I ... I thought ..." I stuttered.

"Yeah, I know, I know." He was flushed and out of breath.

"I saw you going in, little spy mouse." He managed a smile as he shook his sweating head before continuing. "I'll bet Tawdry did too. There's a security camera, you know."

I shrugged, feeling a little stupid but mainly just glad to have escaped Shadowcorps. "She let me out. But I thought you ... I mean I saw you with ... with them and I just figured ..."

"I know." He cut me off. "Those Fiat jokers forced my dad to sell the club to them. They're changing it into the Moulin Noir — how twisted is that? Tonight's the last night as the Moulin D'Or. I tried to talk them out of it today, but I wasted my breath on those weasly wimps. I think Luc might have gone for it, but Louche calls the shots."

"You know them?" I must have sounded stunned.

"Yeah, when I was kid, I'd sneak into the catacombs for fun, and I got to know a lot of the Shadow kids. We never really trusted each other, but I thought it was cool at the time. Luc was okay. He's almost normal, got his mom's aboveground eyes. His slimebucket brother makes up for it with pure creepiness, though."

I told him about the fight I'd witnessed between them. "Wow. Flying glass. A gold cross as a weapon. Cool!"

I told him it hadn't been cool for me, and I was glad to be out of that place. "I'm sorry I misjudged you, Antoine. You really saved me, big time."

"Call me Blag. Antoine sounds so lame. No problem. You gotta lot of nerve, kid." I was about to tell him the rest of what I'd seen in Shadowcorps, but he jumped in. "Anyway, let's save the chatting. This joint's looking a little shaky to me."

He seemed to know his way around as we moved quickly and quietly through the underground. At one point, he stopped and leaned in to whisper to me, "I think I know a way out. I heard some of them talking about this giant ramp set up for the monster crane, whatever that's for. I know where the workshop is, but we'll have to go through town."

I must have looked puzzled, but he just grabbed my sleeve and said, "You'll see. C'mon."

We soon came into blue-lit streets like the ones I'd seen when I'd first climbed down the ladder from the sewer grate. Occasional mini Métros rolled by with their tinted windows. "Check this out." He pointed out a rambling collection of sheds at the end of the passageway. "Les Halles, the real Les Halles."

As we got closer, I could hear the buzz of activity. It was a full-fledged underground market, with merchants at their stalls and Shadow shoppers trying on trench coats, squeezing strange colourless vegetables, and strolling around admiring bony birds hanging from hooks, all the while smoking relentlessly.

Blag leaned into me. "The outdoor market, Les Halles, survived every trashing of Paris for about seven hundred years, but eventually it got torn down too. At night, while it was happening, the Shadows would sneak into the demolition site and steal the remains, bringing them down below to reconstruct the market here. Saved the city a lot of haulage, I figure. No one knew where the piles of smashed sheds went. Voila!" He snorted, sounding sympathetic to the Shadows' cause, as if they'd pulled one over on the big boys this time.

We took a tiny passageway to avoid the shoppers, occasionally dipping into doorways without having to risk discovery. I didn't mind a little break in the terror.

Some things were looking familiar, despite the ever-present stone surfaces, bluish light, and the reek of sewer. Then I realized we were near the giant workroom where I'd seen the crane being assembled. As we peered into the cavernous room, there was activity everywhere. Metal clanged against metal, setting off reverberations in the cavernous room. The low roar of machinery and voices filled the air. Blag looked mesmerized staring at the now completed crane. It was dazzling, with section after section of black gridwork attached together and supported by thick metal girders. A cab for an operator was near one end, with wires extending off in both directions from a pyramid structure that sat on top of the cab. A series of sinister green lights was being tested. To one side lay an enormous hook-like attachment with thick-coiled metal cord wrapped around a cylinder beside it. We were so absorbed in looking at this monstrosity that we almost didn't hear the sound of approaching footsteps. I poked Blag in his considerable chest and hushed him. We ducked out of view as Louche and two of his puffing bullies came into view.

"I'd weep if I could, Louche," laughed one thug.

"Heavy metal heaven," said the other.

"Yesss ... ouiii ... the mini cranes are in place all over the underground, ready for 'lights out.' Every shining monument in Paris will be a memory by tomorrow, my Shadows. But this," he said as he gestured at the metal giant, "this is a work of art."

He turned to one of his cronies. "Did Scar find the little mole?"

"Not yet, Louche. She's probably lost in a slide." The Shadow sounded delighted.

"Ouiii ... yesss ... I suppose. And what could a little Yankee puff of nothing do anyway? Who would believe her story?"

He laughed snidely as they moved on to inspect the finishing touches on the work at hand. Once they were at a distance, Blag tugged my sleeve, and we cautiously made our way past the construction. How could a person Blag's size pass unseen? I wondered. Someone must have read my mind, because just when I thought we were clear and out of view of Louche and the workers, a nasty voice shouted, booming across the immense hollow room. "Hey, there she is! And squarehead's with her. Gargoyles, attack!"

Scar was at the far side of the room and released his pack at that moment.

"Great," Blag spat. "C'mon, kid. Let's hit it."

He grabbed me by an arm, but I didn't need any encouragement. At the far end of the room in the direction we were running was a gigantic platform, and Blag was heading straight for it. The gargoyles would be on us in seconds. Blag was strides ahead of me by then and jumped onto the platform. He pulled a lever on one side, and the whole thing started to tilt upwards toward a set of doors that I could now see beginning to crack open far above. Blag turned back and grabbed me, and we started running up the ramp in the direction of the distant daylight. He held my arm and skipped me like a stone across a lake as he pounded upwards at a remarkable speed, considering his bulk.

The gargoyles were gaining, and I knew we wouldn't make it to the top. In the confusion below, amid a chorus of shouting, Scar was racing toward the ramp as we flew to the opening yawning ahead. As he reached the bottom, he yanked on the lever. The doors started to reverse direction and began to close. The ramp jerked to a halt just as it reached the top and began to lower. Right at this moment, the first of the gargoyles caught up to us and grabbed for me, getting a mouthful of scarf. A rush of terror seized me, and if it weren't for Blag yanking me along, I would've been dinner for six. Blag swung around, unwinding the scarf from my neck then wrapping it around the jaws of the snapping gargoyle. One giant boot to the head later, it tumbled backwards into the pack. Blag stopped briefly to admire his handiwork, but I yelled to him that the ramp was lowering. We hit the top, and he leaped into the shrinking doorway, pushing his beefy body into the crack like the last man onto a crowded métro. I closed my eyes and jumped, grabbing the frame and hoisting myself up at the last second as I looked down at the tumble of gargoyle dogs and the shouting gang below. I squeezed between Blag's legs, and he released the doors, which closed with an awesome jaw-like snap.

Twenty-Two

Blag slumped against the wall of the Shadowcorps building to catch his breath. I was trying to gather my thoughts and recover from the madness we had just left behind. Outside it was a glorious summer day. I'd almost forgotten. It was Bastille Day! The shops were closed and the city was gearing up for a full-on party. So a whole night had passed while I was underground. In some ways it felt like about a month. I should've been tired, completely drained really, but I had this weird, sparkly, energized feeling. Relief, maybe, or hunger. Blag wiped his face with his already soaked T-shirt and gave me a weary look.

"Did you check out that hound mound, Mac? Major league kick-off, huh?"

Thinking about the gargoyles made me shudder. "But I thought they were supposed to be just scary-looking decorations on old churches, like the ones on the Notre Dame cathedral."

Blag nodded seriously. "I've heard of them, never seen one before. When we were kids, the geezers told us stories to try to scare us into not going in the sewers. At the end of the stories, the gargoyles always turned to stone when they hit the daylight." He grinned again. "Man, they were seriously ugly. Anyway, we better beat it before the smokies come lookin' for us."

He looked up at the sky. "'Course, they'd get pretty steamed on a day like this. Supposedly the Shadows can't survive direct sunlight. I've never seen one above ground, except at night, and almost always in the club." Here his face darkened. I supposed he was thinking about the takeover of the Moulin D'Or. He led the way to his cab, which was parked illegally, of course, on the sidewalk. He shredded the parking ticket like confetti and jumped in, opening the passenger door for me from inside. "I'm kinda beat, mind if I go with something a little mellow?" he said, reaching for the stereo, "I'll take you to CAFTA, see if we can find rug-dome there."

I assumed this meant Rudee and thought about having to explain myself to him again. If he'd known what was going to happen with me, he probably would've driven away on that first day at the Pont Neuf. I was glad, recalling my exposure to that cacophonous "Malade" band, to listen to something a little quieter. At that moment, the music started like a cannon shot, and some groaning sounds escaped from the speakers as Blag rolled down all the windows. The bass could have been measured, like earthquakes, on the Richter scale. "Hey, relax, it's a holiday." *Like sunbathing on an airport runway*, I thought.

On the way, Blag seemed to revert to his old self, running lights, screeching to stops, and shaking his Viking action figures at innocent pedestrians, scaring children and their pets with the music thundering out of the windows. I slid down as low as I could in the seat, knowing that since I was sitting in the front, no one would take me for a customer.

All of Paris was in a glowing mood, in contrast to that of my new friend Blag LeBoeuf. It seemed like the city was one giant picnic, with blankets spread out in every available green space that wasn't host to a soccer game of some sort. At one of the fire stations, a fireman was holding a hose pointed in the air while a hundred kids danced in the spray, laughing and yelling. Looked pretty good to me. Even better, though, was when Blag stopped at a crepe stand and bought us the best lunch I've ever had from a street vendor.

When we reached CAFTA, I could see that it was closed but that there was activity inside. I figured it was the Hacks setting up for the big party that night.

"Okay, kid, last stop. It's been a slice. See if you can get cock-a-doodle-Daroo to handle the Louche thing, will you? He's got cop friends, and I don't." This was said with some defiance, but as I climbed out, he grinned at me. "Besides, I gotta go clean up. I've got a date for tonight; think I caught a live one!"

What kind of girl would go for Blag? I mean, he had a good heart, but it would take some serious archaeology to find it. Someone for everyone, I guess. I waved and thanked him again.

Looking through the window of CAFTA, I could see the Hacks hauling their gear onto a little makeshift stage in a corner of the room. Even without hearing them, I could tell that the usual bantering was going on. I knocked at the window. Mink saw me first and must have said something to Rudee, who came running to let me in. "Hey, little Mac, how are you?" he said cheerfully. "You're just in time to help us plug in."

I smiled, wondering if I could hear anything after riding with Blag. I said hi to the other band members. Dizzy waved his trombone slide. "Hey Mac, *ça va?*"

"So, did Sashay give you madeleines and tea all night, *petite?*" asked Rudee. I guessed that was my cover for last night's absence from the church. I realized I couldn't wait. I had to tell Rudee what was going on. This wasn't a secret I wanted to keep. I started slowly. "I know you're not going to be happy about this Rudee, but ..."

That got all their interest. The Hacks put down their instruments and stopped the set-up to hear my story. I had to provide a little background for the others, but for once I had the feeling that they believed me, no matter how far-fetched some of it must have sounded. There were occasional interruptions, but not many, some *oohlala*s and *mon dieus* and much shaking of heads as the tale unfolded. They all agreed that something odd had been going on with the light in Paris lately, and except for Rudee, they'd thought the "Lighten Up" campaign was a joke. Maurice and Henri had heard the gargoyle stories growing up in Toulouse, and Dizzy said he'd seen the Shadows hanging out at an after-hours joint called le Marché Noir, where he'd done a couple of pick-up gigs. They all seemed as shocked at Blag's part in the events as at anything else. Rudee rolled his eyes and curled his lip at the idea of Blag as rescuer, but the part about the closing of the club started him thinking.

"Blag, eh? Well, you can't tell an apple by the core, can you? Sashay had a feeling there were changes coming at the club. Mink, do you still have your hydraulic riser from the Colour Me CooCoo days?"

"Shouldn't be too hard to find. Why, what's on your mind?" Mink rhymed.

"If tonight is Sashay's last show, and the Shadows will all be there, we should make it a night to remember, or for them to forget!"

Rudee laid out his plan to the Hacks, who agreed to help however they could. I think fatigue from last night's craziness was beginning to overcome me, because I started to miss sizeable parts of the conversation, and I began feeling rather foggy. Next thing I knew I was in the back seat of Rudee's cab, comforted by the familiar odour of marinated vegetables, on the way to Sashay's. I woke up for a few moments when she got into the seat beside me and stroked my hair. I remember them talking in hushed tones on the way to the club, but little else.

Outside, the club was draped in a huge banner that read, SOON TO RE-OPEN AS THE MOULIN NOIR, written in gothic script. It was early, so the streets around the club were empty. I noticed Maurice and Henri wheeling something in the back as we arrived at the stage door, then Dizzy pulled up and opened his trunk. Sashay led me into her dressing room and sat me down on a small mountain of silk. She lit some candles and began her preparations at the mirror. I knew she was waiting for me to tell her about my journey to the underground, so I related the tale once more. I could tell she was shocked by some of what she heard, but as always she maintained her air of calm.

"Sorry about losing that beautiful scarf," I said, and she sighed and smiled.

"Mac, will you thank Blag for me? We don't talk...." She shrugged and made one of her famous pouty expressions. "He'll be here tonight, I'm sure. I hope that Rudee's plan will work." She explained what Rudee had in mind. It was a comforting feeling to know that I didn't have to deal with Louche and his foul gang alone again. I was ready to sit back and watch the show.

Twenty-Three

The club was soon filling up for an early show so that everyone could be out in time to catch the Bastille Day fireworks and parties that were planned all over the city. Word had gotten out that this would be Sashay's last appearance, so the nostalgic and curious were out in force. Extra tables were crammed into the balcony section in anticipation of a major Shadow party. The first hint I had of Rudee's plan was when I noticed that some of the regular employees weren't at their usual places. Maurice and Henri, looking very suave with their bulletproof coifs polished to a high gloss, were working together behind the bar, mixing drinks masterfully. Maurice was rhythmically shaking a cocktail mixer over his head while his brother was spinning variously coloured bottles on the bar and pouring two at a time from high above the glasses like a mad scientist. To one side of the stage I spotted

Mink Maynard in a tuxedo uncoiling a microphone cable and checking over some notes. On the other side, Dizzy was laying out some vacuum cleaner–type hose, and we exchanged smiles.

The regular petrified piano player was absent, and in his place was an odd-looking character I didn't recognize, with a long set of gold lamé tails and a too-tall top hat. He was stationed to the left of the stage on a circular riser with velvety material draped around the bottom, at a multi-tiered set of keyboards. He was making last-minute adjustments to a set of pedals when he turned toward Mink side stage to offer a thumbs up. From beneath a silly handlebar moustache, a goofy grin emerged that I recognized right away as belonging to Rudee. The buzz of voices was loud in the club as the Shadows passed through their private entrance to fill the balcony to capacity. Michelle, the cigarette girl, was dispatched with an overflowing tray to take care of their smoking needs, and I was very glad not to be in her place tonight. I'd seen enough of that rancid crew for one lifetime, and I figured they wouldn't be too thrilled to see me.

The lights dimmed, and the crowd quieted in expectation. I saw Henri loading a bunch of glowing greenish drinks onto a tray that was bound for the balcony. A spotlight found Mink Maynard, who strode centre stage, bowed formally, and began his introduction.

"Ladies and gentlemen, *mesdames et messieurs*, a night to remember is yours to be sure. As the curtain falls on the Moulin D'Or and these magic moments will be no more, travel with us to the world of dreams and give yourselves up to the queen. Sail away to childhood's shore with *la Reine des Rêves*, Sashay D'Or!"

His voice rose at the end as the fog from Dizzy's smoke machine seeped into the room, making the floor look like a misty pond at dawn. Rudee began with a low, mysterious wash of chords that floated out of the speakers encircling his riser. The rhythmic blue lights I recalled from the first time I'd experienced Sashay's show were twinkling like soft stars over the crowd, which grew quieter and quieter. Sashay swept onstage in a cascade of silky scarves as Rudee's music rose to meet the moment. Seemingly transported in time herself, Sashay resembled the woman I'd seen on the old Lido poster as she wove her spell on the audience. If not for the ridiculousness of Rudee, I'm sure I would've been caught up in it myself. His riser slowly began to rotate and elevate, adding a dizzy, swirling quality to the music. The smoke machine was working overtime, and Sashay seemed to be floating on waves of foggy satin, back and forth, dipping and spinning, her skirts and scarves overlapping in a golden cascade. The audience was, to say the least, mesmerized.

For once, the Shadows sat in rapt attention as the show reached a majestic climax. Rudee's hands flew over the keyboards. His feet pumped furiously on the pedals and his top hat twirled wildly as his riser ascended and teetered dangerously over the transfixed crowd. Sashay spun like whipped cream, jewelled gloves twirling in time to the spellbinding waves of music. When she finally disappeared in a column of golden mist and the music slowly eased, the audience was transported. Downstairs, happy faces shone like children at play, and laughter flowed through the dreamy crowd.

To my shock, above it all, on the balcony the Shadows were having a wild time of their own. They ran their hands through candles and laughed until their fedoras flew in the air. One was making shadow sharks on the wall while his pals could barely contain themselves, snapping their arms like giant jaws. Another was making rude sounds and causing his trench coat to billow around his bulky body while another had his coat over his head and was racing back and forth on the balcony making ghost sounds. Mink, Dizzy, Maurice, Henri, and Rudee gathered side stage to marvel at the sight.

"Wow," said Dizzy, "what were you playing, Rudee?"

"Ughoman's 'Mesmerata Nocturne,' with a few additions of my own."

Maurice and Henri proudly pointed out the mostly empty glasses of green nectar on the Shadows' tables. "Absinthe makes the heart grow fonder, *non*?" said one brother as the other grinned widely.

Mink coiled up his mike cable and laughed. "And how about Sashay's dance? That should chill their nasty plans."

Suddenly a door slammed loudly backstage, and a rush of footsteps was heard in the hall. Through the doors to the kitchen burst Louche, followed by Scar and Phlegm. They stopped just inside the club and stared at the action on the balcony, momentarily stunned by what they saw. "Scar, hit the lights and cut that smoke machine. Phlegm, round up those losers, now. We've got a night's work to do," barked Louche.

He was, if possible, even unhappier than he had been during the fight with his brother. The Hacks and I concealed ourselves backstage, wondering how this was going to play out, and Rudee rushed to Sashay's dressing room. Louche strode across the room like a prison warden who's just stopped an escape attempt. The Shadow play ended abruptly, and they hastily grabbed hats, coats, and smokes and unsteadily made their way out the private exit. Scar joined Louche and Phlegm on the balcony. They conferred briefly, one picking up a nearly empty glass of green liquid and sniffing it before slamming the glass down and smashing it on the table. Louche shot a look back toward the stage over the heads of the confused patrons, seeming to scan the area for suspects. He then violently kicked over a table, scattering the contents, and exited to join his departed thugs.

I left the other Hacks and went backstage to find Rudee, where I bumped right into Blag in the dim hallway. It was like walking into a wall. "Sorry. Oh Blag, I'm glad to see you." I fumbled for words.

"So this was Daroo's big idea? Bore the smokies stiff with his feeble tunes and some dry ice? This was supposed to get them out of the way, then everything would go happily ever after? Does he drink his own drool for breakfast?"

"Blag, I know it didn't work, but I've got an idea. Can you take me to Madeleine's office?"

"Sure kid, but this better have more juice than Daroo's cheeseball show. C'mon, my car's in the alley. I doubt we have much time."

Twenty-Four

The streets were clogged with Bastille Day revellers, but my mind was racing as Blag's cab crawled through the crowds up the hill to Montmartre. Flags were flying from every building, and parades of all sizes wound their way along sidewalks full of people. Kids in painted faces, musicians, jugglers, dancers, and dogs in ridiculous costumes all added to the happy feeling of a summer celebration. The local fire halls were decorated with flowers and streamers for the evening's dances. Slumped in the seat beside a silent Blag, who for once seemed to have forgotten his ear-shattering music collection, I felt it was up to me to devise a plan to stop Louche's Bastille Day nightmare. Maybe Rudee, together with the Hacks and Sashay, had slowed things down a little by distracting the Shadows, but I knew it wasn't enough. And the police, the ones who were supposed to prevent this kind of madness, what about them? If Magritte, nice enough to be sure, was an example of the art of crime prevention, then Paris had some dark days ahead.

"Okay, Cal Gal, this is it. Want me to hang in?"

Blag indicated the old stone tower that served as Madeleine's office on a street behind the Sacre Coeur church. There was a bright light shining on the top floor. "If you don't mind. I have to talk to Madeleine, but I really need your help."

"Yeah, alright, but I'm not going up. She's still lathered about me cranking up Malade and cruising past the Pope during his speech. Can you believe it?"

Looking for the stairs, instead I found a ramp that wound to the top of the tower. From above I could hear the crackle of the taxi radio system and occasionally Madeleine's voice barking out instructions. I called up, "Madeleine? Hello? It's me, Rudee's friend Mac."

"Ah, little Mac, come up, *ma petite*. I've been waiting to meet you."

The top of the ramp opened onto a circular room that overlooked all of Paris. The view was majestic. Madeleine swung around from her microphone at the centre of a large console, featuring an electronic map of the city, and waved me over with a giant smile. Then I noticed her wheelchair and understood the need for the ramp.

Up close, she was a pudding of happy wrinkles and silver hair springing in random directions. She planted a couple of gooey, ruby-coloured kisses on my cheeks and looked me over. "Ahh, but you're just *une jeune fille*, aren't you? Here."

She handed me a bowl of strawberries, and I couldn't say no. "What do you think of my chariot? This year's model, *mes chauffeurs* bought it for me for Christmas."

Madeleine indicated her gleaming wheelchair and proceeded to give me a demonstration of its impressive moves, gliding back and forth across her little room, spinning and stopping effortlessly. "I can see by your face that you have more on your mind than a little visit, *ma petite*. What is it?"

I drew in a deep breath and started my story once more, not wanting to waste time, and hoping she'd believe a tale that sounded crazy even to me. "Madeleine, do you know where all your drivers are, and can you contact them at any time?"

"*Bien sur*, of course," she replied and wheeled over to her map, which showed a system of little orange lights moving through every part of Paris. "*Les voila*, and I feel like I can almost see them out of my window on the world. Beautiful, *non*?"

It was indeed glorious, but I couldn't stop to admire the view.

"Do you have access to other information on your map ... like the entrances to the sewer system?"

She smiled at me, swung her chair around with a tiny whirr, and tapped on a keyboard until a different set of lights showed up on the map. I rushed through my story and the plan that was formulating as I went along. There was no time to lose. Within twenty minutes, a cluster of cabs was gathering at the top of Montmartre in a jumble that must have blocked any attempt at passage through the area, although I doubted if anyone cared in the city that night. I could hear the laughter and music pouring out of windows everywhere as I ran into the midst of the drivers. Madeleine's voice cut through the night air on a couple hundred cab radios.

"Listen, *mes amis*. Tonight, Paris needs us for much more than our wheels. The city needs our hearts, our courage, and all the light that we have to shine into some very dark places. Listen to little Miss Mac and then make me proud, *mes chauffeurs*."

I climbed up on one trombone-shaped exhaust pipe, and Dizzy hoisted me up on top of his cab, as all the drivers stood beside their cars to listen. Just as I finished, our heads all turned at once to witness the first burst of crackling fireworks filling the July sky above the Trocadero. A city-wide cheer had erupted and was rolling like a wave from window to window when suddenly all the lights in the city went out.

Twenty-Five

The sky was alive with flashes of colour and exploding pinwheels. All the customary oohing and ahhhing accompanied each new starburst, and it seemed that the city was oblivious to the fact that every light in Paris had been extinguished. Either that or they thought it was part of the show. I knew differently; it meant that Louche had successfully begun his "lights out" plan. I also knew what was to follow and that the moment for action was now. In the confusion of the blackout, the cabbies jumped into their cars as Madeleine began her rapid-fire instructions.

"Forty-three. Place de Clichy. Rue Amsterdam. Nineteen. Rue d'Alsace, Gare de L'Est. One twenty-three. Boulevard Montparnasse. La Coupole."

I slid off Dizzy's car and grabbed Rudee's sleeve as he was scanning the darkened square looking for me. "Hey, Mac. Jump in." He headed for the driver's side door, but I didn't get in.

"Rudee, can you find Jerome and have him round up the river rats? They'll have flares on the boats, and we'll need all the light we can get."

It was then that I noticed Sashay huddled in the back of Rudee's car. He must have been taking her home when the call went out. She lifted her head when she heard my voice and beckoned to me. She unwrapped a layer of her outfit and handed me a dazzling white scarf that I recognized from the show. "Here, *ma cherie*, I'm sure you'll put it to better use than I did."

I mumbled a thanks, giving the scarf a carefree toss around my neck as she had shown me, and Sashay couldn't help but smile. "Rudee, I'll meet you at the *bouquinistes*. Go ahead."

He didn't look too happy with this idea but closed his door anyway and started backing out of the tangle of cabs. I found Blag, as usual, by himself, parked with his engine rumbling, by the curb.

"We've got to deal with that cloud tank I told you about. Any ideas, Blag?" I called in his window. He got out and grinned as he popped the trunk. Inside was the biggest portable stereo I'd ever seen, with speakers the size of small refrigerators. He slammed the trunk and off we sped. The streets were lit on and off by the glow of the ongoing fireworks, and the cheering at each new blast from the Trocadero seemed more and more bizarre when I thought about where we were heading. I could see cabbies at various places along the way positioning their cars, awaiting Madeleine's signal. "How will we get in?" I asked, realizing that I also had no idea how to find my way to the lab in Shadowcorps once we did get in.

"Don't worry, I've got connections," he replied, giving me a knowing look.

We slammed to a halt at almost the exact spot we'd emerged from after our underground adventure the night before. Blag hauled the massive blaster from the trunk and quickly flipped through his music collection.

"Tonnage. Yeah. 'Demolition Dance.' That should do it. C'mon."

Sure enough, Blag punched in the code, and the shining black doors of Shadowcorps opened immediately for us. We took the elevator down five flights, and when we emerged, it was eerily quiet. I don't know what I'd expected to hear, but it wasn't silence. Not on this night. We raced past the workshop where the giant crane had been assembled. Gone. Except for some tools, welders' visors, and the usual carpet of butts lying around, the room was empty. It gave me a sick feeling, but we had work to do. Blag led us right to the doors of the inner sanctum of Shadowcorps and buzzed the security button.

"Black mamba. Ready or not, here we camba." The doors hissed open, and there was Tawdry doing some repairs to a spike heel that looked like a surgical instrument. "Shouldn't you be waxing your whiskers, pussycat?" asked Blag with a gleam in his eye. Was she his connection?

"I'm sure you're right, my funky chunk. I'd better beat it before the fireworks start underground."

She smiled at me, blew Blag a pouty kiss, and reattached her high heel. She directed us down one of the plush hallways. We proceeded quickly but cautiously. Blag balanced the blaster on one shoulder like it was a pocketbook. It looked to me like a shipping trunk with dials. We arrived at the lab and listened at the door. All I could hear, aside from the bubbling of little sparks in the cloud tank, was the sound of lips smacking and uncontrolled chewing. The doctor must be building up his strength for his big show tonight, I thought. Blag gave me a silent questioning expression, and I motioned for him to move down the hall a little ways. I tapped on the door, and using my lowest delivery guy voice, said, "Dr. Brouillard. Gift basket delivery for Dr. Etienne Brouillard. There's a hindquarter of steer at reception. We'll need a signature to deliver it, doctor."

I looked at Blag, and he turned his substantial back to me, but I could see his shoulders shaking with silent laughter. I stepped aside just in time as the doors whipped open and the doctor burst into the hallway, rushing toward reception. He seemed oblivious to the disappearance of the delivery person, and Blag stood watching in amazement before turning to me. "Moves pretty quickly for a large man. Hey, nice voice ... just kidding. Let's go to work."

"All right, funky chunk," I laughed.

He stopped for a few seconds to admire his target then found a plug for his stereo before setting it up on the conference table directly in front of the tank. Inside, the tiny clouds danced happily in their glowing patterns awaiting their release. Blag handed me a set of foam earplugs, and we stepped to the side of the blaster as he hit "play." I felt like I was inside a thunderclap or at the centre of a sonic boom as the music, or whatever that sound was, began and seconds later the tank shattered into a thousand flying pieces. Blag pulled me behind him, and we ducked beneath the table as the air was filled first with fragments of glass then with tiny floating specks of dewy light. Blag stood for a few moments, bobbing his head in time to Tonnage, then hastily unplugged his stereo and threw it onto his shoulder. "You didn't think I was leaving this baby behind, did ya? We better bolt, kiddo."

As we reached the door I took a quick glance back and stopped him. "Hey, look." Each tiny speck of light had formed into a perfect miniature cloud and was raining on the spot directly below it in the conference room.

"And me without an umbrella," chortled Blag, and off we went down the hall. The sound of approaching shouting voices forced us to duck into a smaller hallway that crossed the main one.

"I don't have a clue. It sounded like it came from the lab, Louche." I recognized the always-friendly tones of Phlegm.

"Something's wrong," came the reply from the boss. "Scar, call the mini crane crews. Tell them we start immediately. Phlegm, have the gargoyles accompany the Shadows. They'll love the darkness."

Louche sounded more tense than ever. I wished I could've seen his expression when he saw the mess in the lab. Then there was the sound of running footsteps coming up from behind them.

"Hey, wait. Hey." It was the doctor, very out of breath, and seriously agitated. "Have any of you seen a gift basket with a hindquarter of steer?"

"Zip it, porky. You're in the brine for this," snapped Phlegm.

"You're not going to like this, Louche," growled Scar from further down the hall.

"My clouds!" screamed the doctor. "Who let them out? It isn't time."

"Give the order," spat Louche in his most venomous tone, "open the grates. Lights out! And when I find out who did this ..."

Blag and I didn't wait to hear the rest. In the confusion, as tiny clouds filled the hall, we escaped quickly past the now vacant reception desk. We took the quickest way possible through the deserted workshop and up to the street. I was completely winded and could barely get my words out. "Blag ... we have to call Madeleine ... tell her to ... give the signal. I think those mini cranes are going ... after every monument in Paris."

"You're right, nana, and in this darkness, who's going to stop them?" he added grimly.

Twenty-Six

Madeleine must have still been organizing the cabbies, because Blag couldn't get through on the radio. "Line's jammed, Mac, but I'll keep trying," he said as he glanced over at me with one hand on the wheel. Sharing the front seat of Blag's cab was like being in a crowded elevator.

In a few minutes we crossed the Pont Neuf, and I spotted Rudee with Jerome at his *bouquiniste* stand. A gang of river rats was forming around them. Blag spat out his window in disgust. "Daroo's got some tasty friends. Where did he dredge that crew up from, the bottom of the Seine?"

I ignored him, but I could see where he was coming from. The river rats were tattered, had skipped bathtime once or twice, and were maybe missing some teeth, but I figured we weren't going to dinner at Le Dome. I was just about to jump out when Blag called out excitedly,

"Hey, the line's open. I've got her. Hang on, Mad. What next, kid?"

"Tell her to give the signal as soon as everyone's in place," I shouted as I rushed over to the growing collection of river rats gathered around Jerome's stand. Each had a torch in one hand, and, as if they had rehearsed it, they then put them all into the centre of the group as Jerome lit a match. The flame leapt from one to the next rapidly, and the street corner lit up like we'd started a bonfire.

At that moment Rudee called to me over the sound of the noisy crowd of river rats. "Mac, look down, beside the river below the bridge. What's that machine with those people on it? Are my eyes dreaming?"

From a grate beneath the Pont Neuf on the other side of the river, a small black crane had emerged that was only now dimly visible in the torchlight. The arm was extending in the direction of the statue of Henri IV. Rudee and I jumped into his cab and raced across the darkened bridge as the river rats began to make their way down to the edge of the Seine, torches in hand. Once we got to the other side of the bridge, Rudee turned sharply and headed down a ramp clearly not meant for cars. Just then, the radio crackled, and Madeleine's voice burst through the sound of wheels bouncing wildly.

"Alright, *mes chauffeurs*. Everyone together now. Lighten up!" As she called out the planned signal, all over Paris the headlamps of taxis came blazing to life, pointing into sewer grates and shining into the openings to the underground. The river rats could be seen fanning out alongside the river, beaming their torches into crevices known only to them and the few others who inhabited the darker corners of the city. Rudee jumped a barrier, and his bumper gave a nauseating scraping sound before dangling like a broken wing from his car, as we bounced dangerously over cobblestones toward the edge of the river. He swung around and headed along a narrow path, sometimes on two wheels, in the direction of the crane, silhouetted against the night sky. We came screeching to a halt, almost skidding into the Seine as he hit the high beams, illuminating a chilling sight.

Stunned at the controls of the crane was a Shadow in a hardhat with his arm up trying to block the glare of Rudee's headlights. The crane's hook was dangling inches from Henry IV, who seemed unmoved by the imminent danger. With the cab lights keeping the Shadow from his dirty work, Rudee and I leapt out of the car and ran toward the opening to the sewer under the bridge. A large rusty grate was lying on the ground, and emerging from the darkness we saw a group of Shadows, one driving an empty mining cart, presumably meant for Henry IV, and behind him another with snarling gargoyles on a leash. I couldn't see Rudee's expression in this light, but my own experience with these monsters came rushing back to me, and I froze. Why had we been in such a rush to peer into the depths of Paris? We were in complete darkness, and the cab lights weren't going to help us now. I could make out the shape of a flapping trench coat and fedora just barely holding the beasts back, then I heard a chilling voice I recognized too well. "There she is. Grab the kid. Forget the joker with her."

Out of all the sewer entrances in Paris, why did I have to choose the same one as Scar? Just then a couple of river rats with torches raced down the ramp in our direction. *Just in time*, I thought, but then Scar released one of the gargoyles, and it flew at me like a foaming panther. I saw the horror on Rudee's face in the approaching torchlight as the beast snatched me by my coat, lifted me in the air like a morsel of prey and carried me back to Scar. At the thug's instruction, the gargoyle deposited me in the mining cart, which immediately began retreating back underground into the darkness.

As I looked back, wiping foam from my collar, I could make out the river rats and Rudee racing toward the shrinking hole behind me. One of the Shadows was doubled over, shielding his eyes from the torchlight, and the gargoyle at his side appeared to be frozen as stiff as a snow sculpture. Scar jumped on to the edge of the cart and pushed off into the blackness below. The reek of the sewer came from his breath as he leaned within inches of my face.

"You'll make the perfect little Bastille Day gift for Louche. Hang on, little troublemaker."

I would have closed my eyes, but I couldn't see anything anyway. It was like a roller coaster out of control, hurtling straight down into complete darkness. We made sudden lurches to one side then the other, and one hideous bump left us in midair for what seemed like days. Scar coughed out a cackling laugh when we bounced back onto the cart's wheels again. When we finally hit bottom, chaos greeted us. Cranes were backing up and trying to turn around in the darkened passageways, and Shadows were stumbling with their hands across their eyes, cursing and bumping into each other.

I allowed myself a moment of pleasure as it occurred to me that the lights from Madeleine's drivers, together with the river rats' torches, must have driven the Shadows back where they came from. The blue lights embedded in the stone walls of the underground were flickering madly, and many were dead completely. I guessed that the power failure must have had its effect down here as well. Scar quickly took in the surrounding mess and grabbed me, dragging me down a foul-smelling passage away from the chaos.

Twenty-Seven

The level of the rank-smelling sewer water rose as we headed farther away from the mad scene behind us. The stone walls of the passage were increasingly covered in a grey fungus that fought for space with the dangling spiderwebs that swayed above as we hurried by. More than once, Scar angrily flicked bits of web from his face, muttering. There was clearly no one following us, but he kept looking back anyway, and he paused as we reached a neat pile of skulls stacked like blocks in a recessed section of stone. I recoiled when he lifted the jaw of the topmost skull and reached inside it. At this, the stack of empty heads swung to one side like the devil's garden gate, and we plunged into yet another level of darkness. Either those ashy eyes could penetrate the dark, or he was very familiar with the place, because Scar whisked along the winding paths.

The sewer smell was fading, and its place was taken by a salty mineral odour. The dampness was even more present than usual, and the temperature was rising. I loosened Sashay's scarf so that I could breathe a bit more easily. Then Scar passed through a rounded arch just ahead and stopped to snap on his mirror glasses. A large room with a domed ceiling lay before us with walls of huge amber stones, and there were smoking pots everywhere. A series of long, smooth marble steps led to a steaming pool that was decorated at the edges with carvings of people in flowing robes, some with dogs' or horses' heads, some with wings for arms. A chubby stone violinist with curly hair dominated the centre of the pool and a fountain of water flowed from the head of his instrument into the steam below. The only sound was the bubbling of the pool. This was the source of the mineral smell, now almost overpowering.

In a hesitant, almost hushed tone, Scar finally spoke to the bubbles. "Boss? Louche? Sorry to bother you, but ..."

A voice responded from the cauldron of steam below, and I could just make out the shape of a head seeming to rise disembodied from the warm fog. "Yessss, ouiii ... welcome, little mole. Few have seen this place, and then only Shadows. What do you think?" He seemed to be wheezing steam.

"Louche, uh I've gotta tell you ..." Scar interrupted before Louche cut him off.

"Roman, little one, but I suppose for you

ancient history would be the lunar landing, or maybe Woodstock."

Scar was twitching like he had to go to the little Shadows' room. His voice was nervous, but he persisted. "Louche, it's all gone up in smoke. The lights out plan. The clouds, the mini cranes, all of it. Once they access emergency power, it'll be back to the city of light as usual."

"Yessss, ouiii, Scar. Breathe. Have a smoke. Relax, a drink perhaps."

Louche gestured toward a large corked bottle of black liquid resting in a stone holder at his side, and his teeth gleamed into a slit of a smile. I recognized the bottle from my first visit to the lab but tried not to focus on it too long.

"Sure, boss," laughed Scar nervously, sounding a little more like his old nasty self.

"Fear not, the underworld will rule when the time is right," Fiat went on dreamily.

I could feel a speech coming on with lots of cheesy references to dark destiny, the true Paris, and maybe even his great-great-grandmother's birthday cake, so I risked an interruption. "Look, Louche, you could return the monuments, no real harm's been done. A good lawyer, a full confession, you're maybe looking at a suspended sentence, some community service erasing graffiti in the Métro, I don't know." It was desperate, and he wasn't buying it, but I kept going. "There's no need to keep me here. I won't mention this place, you know, your Roman sauna, or whatever you call it."

This seemed to have the opposite effect on him, and he hissed his reply. "I may be mad, but I'm not stupid, little one. Nor am I finished, despite what my smoky associates believe, either. You see, unlike my dim bulb of a brother, I could never live above ground, not that I would want to in that baguette-and-brie mall they call a city. Scar, my robe."

Scar handed Louche a black toga as he emerged from the steaming liquid. I caught a glimpse of his greyish, perfectly smooth shoulders and chest before looking away, hoping to find a quick exit. Scar, anticipating this, was soon back at my side. "Louche, what do you want me to do with the twerp?" he rasped, lighting up and blowing smoke at me.

"Nothing, *mon flou*. She will be my accomplice in a final, albeit symbolic act that the darkness will allow us, the sweet desecration of the soul of the city, Notre Dame de Paris."

While I was trying to sort out what this meant and how I could possibly be regarded as an accomplice, he slipped into an adjacent room and emerged minutes later, dressed in a tight-fitting black outfit, with gloves and hood to match.

Scar led the way out of Louche's private Roman bath, which was extraordinary, I had to admit. My curiosity got the better of me. "How come nobody knows about this place? It looks like an archaeologist's dream."

Louche eyed me with suspicion but replied anyway, "Ouiiii ... quite right, little wisp. The Crypte Archéologique is right next door, with its admirable

Roman ruins, but they stopped excavation before finding the real treasure for fear of weakening the foundation of the great cathedral. At least, that was the reason given in my brother's report to the city."

He narrowed his eyes, and a most sinister look came over his face. "But tonight, a new chapter will be added to the history of Notre Dame. Yesss, something added ..." he paused and snarled "... and something taken away. Let's go."

Twenty-Eight

Louche led the way through an entrance like a sewer pipe, in which we all had to crouch as we walked, into the Crypte Archéologique. It held a very stylish presentation of Roman ruins with historical maps of the original site and photos on the walls that I couldn't make out in the dimness. We came out on the street in front of Notre Dame. The Place du Parvis, normally crowded with tourists, souvenir hustlers, and business people having lunch, was empty. In the deep darkness that the power outage had thrown the city into, the shape of the magnificent cathedral was more dramatic than ever. A few people walked the streets, but most seemed to have headed indoors to party by candlelight. Those that were out ignored us as we moved down the street bordering the cathedral, watched by the ominous stone gargoyles leaning over the sides of the building. As we rounded the corner and entered the Place Jean XXIII, my heart stopped beating for a moment when I saw Louche's destination.

Before me was the biggest construction crane I'd ever seen, looming like a giant steel dinosaur in the stillness of the park. If possible, it looked larger and more powerful than when I'd seen it being constructed in the underground workshop of Shadowcorps. Louche crossed the square to the base of the crane in seconds, and I had no choice but to follow with Scar urging me from behind, one grisly hand on my arm the whole time in case I had any thoughts of skipping the festivities.

Louche must have had some spider blood in him, because he quickly scaled the ladder that led to the operator's cab, champagne bottle in hand. I was in no hurry to follow, but Scar, who remained on the ground, wasn't open to discussing the matter. I'd seen enough ladders for a lifetime, but this one was downright disturbing as I made my way up into the black Parisian night sky. A breeze from the river below turned the July night a few degrees chillier, and I tugged Sashay's scarf gratefully around my neck. Louche had already reached the metal crow's nest and was opening the door while I was barely a quarter of the way up.

With too much time to think and too far to fall, the events of the past week turned in my mind in a dizzy playback. I'd gotten into a lot of this on my own through a combination of foolishness and good intentions, and we know where those will take you. My hands were turning sweaty, and I had an increasingly hard time clinging to the cold black metal of the crane's ladder. Once my sneaker missed a step. I lunged for the next rung and clung to it with my heart and head pounding. I remember thinking that this would be a bad time to faint. I concentrated on my life at home in California, my parents, friends, and school until I could make my breathing regular again. It was one thing to save Paris from "eternal midnight," as Louche called it, but it was a whole other to think about not seeing Upper Mandeville again. I pushed myself upwards, concentrating on one rung, one breath at a time.

Reaching out of the little door, Louche grabbed me by my coat and hauled me into the little box in the sky. "Beats the Roue de Paris any time, *non, ma petite*?" he laughed viciously.

He had the lights on the crane's dashboard illuminated and seemed to be reviewing the controls. He flipped over a key and the engine jumped to life, shuddering and shaking the driver's cab like a box of bolts. The green glow from the controls reflected off Louche's phantom gaze, and I saw him for the true madman that he was.

From below, no sound reached us, and all I could see was the silhouette of the city's skyline, jagged with rooftops and chimneys, the dark-flowing River Seine to one side and the colossal shape of Notre Dame on the other. Candlelight twinkled in the city's windows as Bastille Day had gone indoors for the night, spirits dimmed but no doubt not defeated. A thundering lurch that made the ones on the Ferris wheel feel like soft caresses shook the cab as Louche kicked the full power on for the main boom of the crane, and it began to swing in the direction of the church.

Scar, alone in the square beneath us, began waving his arms like he was trying to taxi in a jumbo jet, but I'm almost sure Louche paid him no attention. He seemed completely intoxicated by his power over the hulking device as he engaged the gears with an ugly grind and turned, rolling across the square toward the cathedral. He was so pumped up, he was unable to sit any longer and planted himself with one hand on the wheel like a crazed bronco rider. I sat dumbly at his side, not daring to move or spend too much time looking down, trying to guess his ultimate goal but gradually sensing where he was heading.

The giant hook hanging from the end of the crisscross steel limb swung like a possessed pendulum as the arm arched over the famous flying buttresses of Notre Dame toward the grand spire that dominated the night sky. *Impossible, ridiculous* I thought, but then I realized it didn't matter to a man who'd lost whatever fragile grasp of reality he'd had left when this episode began. His grandiose scheme had been shut down, but he was reacting like a mosquito had annoyed him. His brother had, in his mind, betrayed him; and all of his plans, except this last one, were history.

One more grinding metallic shudder, and Louche bounced in place like a cartoon fool. I could see that the crane had found its destination. As he'd said himself, he might be mad, but he was not stupid. He had calmed down enough to zero in on fine-tuning the claw above its majestic prey when I saw something in the dull blur of the city that caught my eye. Tiny dots of light, in pairs, were moving in and out of sight, but gradually making their way toward the Isle de la Cité and Notre Dame.

The cabbies! Madeleine's chauffeurs must have abandoned their stations at the openings to the underground, having driven the Shadows into retreat, and were now zooming en masse toward the scene of Louche's ultimate crime in action. He, on the other hand, was so preoccupied with perfecting the placement of the crane's giant arm and swinging hook that he clearly hadn't noticed.

"Aha!" he yelled triumphantly as the hook found its way around the top of the spiky spire of Notre Dame. He was reaching for a large lever on the floor, which I'm certain would have started to separate the spire from the roof of the cathedral. I shouted "No!" and pushed him as hard as I could. I'm not that strong, but the unexpected thrust while he was engaged in his task must have taken him by surprise, because he bounced across the cab, knocking the door open and falling partway out into the night air. In an act of pure reflex, I reached out to stop him from tumbling to the ground, and he snatched my hand, yanking himself back in. If I expected gratitude, I got fury, and he turned back to the controls just as a crossfire of light from the square below pinned him in place. In the glare I could see the cabs gathering beneath us, some with their front wheels on the trunks of others, some on makeshift ramps, all shining up in the direction of the crane and illuminating Louche's desperate enterprise.

After only a moment's hesitation, Louche grabbed his bottle and blindly leaped from the cab. I watched, horrified, as he jumped onto the arm of the crane and raced in the direction of the roof of the cathedral. In the time since, I've had many opportunities to try to answer the question of why I did what I did, but I still don't really know for sure. Was it bravado or some overdeveloped sense of responsibility that pulled me out of the crane's cab? I mean, what's the worst that he could have done with a bottle of black paint and a wild glint in his eye? Maybe the altitude affected my judgment — I don't know. I do know that I followed Louche down the length of the boom, not as quickly as his spider-like motion took him, but I didn't stop to take in the sights either.

When he reached the end of the crane's huge arm, Louche stopped to look back and seemed momentarily stunned to see me following him. "If I can't steal it, I can stain it forever," he shouted in the blaze of taxi lights that caught him like a soloist in a spotlight. He was about to race away, but then he turned back and called out more calmly, "You're over your head, little one. Go back while you still can." With that, he grabbed the rope with a gloved hand, the bottle still in the other, and slid like a crazed swashbuckler down the cable to the hook that dangled below.

I don't remember thinking about turning back, but I must have had a moment's pause, because I recall looking down and seeing Rudee racing madly across the square, arms and hair flapping frantically. I knew I couldn't let my attention be pulled toward the ground, but I also realized quickly that Louche's downward route wasn't available, even if I wanted to brave it. He hit the roof of the church and grabbed the crane's hook, pulling it backwards then flinging it with all his strength out into the night. The wild sway made climbing down the cable impossible and the thought of staying on the rocking steel tentacle very scary. Fear is a strange feeling and quite useful at certain times. It focuses everything in you on one thing; I guess some would say survival. I don't know. We haven't started psychology yet at school.

Thought? Instinct? Pure lunacy? I don't know what did it, but I unwrapped Sashay's scarf from my neck and opened it fully. I grabbed the corners, allowing it to billow out above my head, and closed my eyes. The sweet smell of freesias in my mom's garden wafted up to meet me. The sound of the lazy summer bees and crickets filled the cool air around me. Then I landed. Owwww! My ankle! The spiky roof of Notre Dame de Paris pierced my skinny little body *and* my childhood reverie, and I looked around. Louche had turned and spotted me in disbelief, but he held his black champagne defiantly over his head.

"It's over, Louche. Look!" I gestured to the scene below where the river rats, torches in hand, could be seen weaving their way up from the edges of the Seine toward the heart and soul of Paris on the Isle de la Cité. Behind them it seemed like every Bastille Day reveller in the city had decided to follow and join the midnight parade. Suddenly the streets were filled with people yelling, cheering, carrying candles, lighters, flashlights, whatever illumination that could be found.

Louche looked around wildly, as if expecting help. "Gargoyles, attack! Gargoyles, now! Scar, call the gargoyles. What are you waiting for?" He screamed into the night, but the stone monsters that have guarded Notre Dame for hundreds of years refused to abandon their posts. He swung his bottle above his head, calling out a final desperate "Lights out, Paris!" I ran at him across the rooftop, and I could hear the crowd, cheering or swooning as the wind caught my scarf. I didn't want to let go of my security blanket, Sashay's silky accessory, and it enveloped the two of us in a dizzy rooftop dance that the queen of dreams would have marvelled at. I watched as the bottle, seemingly in slow motion, flew from Louche's hand into the sky above us, and he and I staggered, twisted around a few times then ended up dangling over the square far below, before all the lights of Paris came back on at once.

Twenty-Nine

Minutes or hours later, I couldn't tell you which, we were surrounded by police and officials who had us disentangled, pulled to safety, and separately dealt with. Louche was unceremoniously hauled off while I was treated like a visiting angel. An easier way down was found through the inside of the cathedral, which I'm sorry to say I wasn't able to appreciate, and I was reunited with the jubilant band of cabbies in the square outside.

With his snowplough brow leading the way, Rudee shot toward me with that parental mixture of total anxiety and complete relief. He scooped me up in his arms and lifted me off the ground just when I was getting used to being on earth again. Then he planted me in front of him, hands firmly on my shoulders as if he was afraid that I might fly away. He seemed on the verge of tears.

"Little Mac! I was worried as a warthog, but now I'm happy as pig!"

"Hey, nice landing, little one." Dizzy was grinning beside him, and added, "Rudee, I like 'happy as pig,' maybe it's the title for our album."

Mink Maynard added, "Yeah, that's cool. It's only for you I flip my wig, baby you make me happy as pig."

Rudee shot Mink a look but couldn't help laughing. I spotted the gleaming domes of Maurice and Henri in the cluster of drivers standing around their cars and talking excitedly. A spontaneous party was starting to break out in the square. The river rats were improvising a torch dance, and the people who'd spilled into the street were stomping and clapping and joining in. There was no sign of Blag, so I figured he was trying to turn a little profit now that light had returned to the streets of Paris, and with it some potential customers.

Just then I noticed, in the middle of the river rats' midnight mayhem, a statue I hadn't seen before. Instead of the usual cracked grey stone, it was wet, a dull black in colour, and represented a man looking up, trying to shield his eyes, in a fedora and trench coat. There was broken glass at his feet. Strange.

I fell into the back seat of Rudee's cab, exhausted, but too fired up to rest. Madeleine's voice came over the radio. "Bravo, *mes chauffeurs*. You've made me proud, as I knew you would. And a thousand *mercis* to Mademoiselle Mac, our little angel from California."

A chorus of honking horns greeted this announcement, and I sank into the seat, embarrassed but unable to hide my smile from Rudee, who was grinning back at me in the mirror. "It's never too late to celebrate. Let the Bastille Day party at CAFTA begin!" roared Madeleine.

"Some beet borscht before we put on the party pants, little one?"

I was about to show my disgust for Rudee's taste in food, but then I realized he was kidding. He spotted an all-night cafe that was back in action with the relighting of the city, and I waited while he ran in for some much-needed sandwiches. I devoured my snack as Rudee drove, and when he crossed the Pont Notre Dame, I looked back at the Gothic cathedral, now framed by the lights of the city. All was as it had been before tonight, for centuries unchanged, the towers arching proudly into the sky, the beautiful flying buttresses, the mysterious stone gargoyles, and the mighty spire. All were where they should be. It already seemed like a dream.

When we pulled up in front, CAFTA was alive like I'd never seen it. The streets surrounding the café were jammed with cabs, other cars, and motorcycles, so Rudee stopped when he couldn't go any farther and jumped out. I guessed that no one would be going anywhere for a while. At first, when we entered, nobody even noticed us in the general craziness that was building in the room. Then we were spotted and met with cheers.

"*Bonsoir*, little angel. When did you grow your wings?"

"Hey, Rudee, who's the little parachutist?"

"Bravo, Mademoiselle Mac!"

To use my dad's expression, I worked the room, thanking all the drivers for coming to my rescue and spotlighting my crane acrobatics. They had some pretty amazing stories themselves about the throngs of Shadows that had come bursting like clouds of vapour from the sewers, ready to do their worst with their mini cranes and their snarling beasts. It seemed that gargoyles came in all shapes, and the drivers exchanged stories about giant crow-shaped ones, cat-like creatures with no tails, and an assortment of really ugly dog gargoyles.

By the time Rudee and I arrived, the other members of the Hacks were finishing their last minute stage set-up in the corner and were nearly ready to play. Maurice was resining up the bow of his bass, and I wondered if he used the same stuff on his hair. Henri was leaning over his banjo, trying hard to tune over the hubbub of the cafe. I saw that Dizzy had fixed a French tricolour flag to the end of the slide on his trombone, and Mink was chatting up a woman in the audience, no doubt dazzling her with rhyme.

Just then, the crowd parted to make way for two very serious-looking gendarmes. *Surely*, I thought, *they're not going to shut down the party before the Hacks play their first note*. They pressed through the partygoers toward the stage, and I noticed a familiar figure between them in a black tailored coat and bowler hat, carrying his usual rolled umbrella. Even on a national holiday, Magritte kept his look intact. I supposed that if he'd been in a Hawaiian shirt, no one would have recognized him.

He leaned up to Rudee, who was by then on stage, and said something to him. Rudee reached out a hand and helped the little man up onto the stage. "*Mes amis*," shouted Rudee over the crowd, "before the Hacks begin to rock the CAFTA" — a cheer greeted this suggestion — "We have a VIP with us, a very impeccable policeman." More cheering and laughter followed this remark. "I give you Inspecteur Magritte!"

If for no other reason, his overall tidiness brought Magritte respect, and the crowd quieted somewhat. "I come tonight to say *merci* on behalf of all of Paris to you, *les chauffeurs*." Magritte inclined his head and touched his bowler in respect as a thunderous cheer erupted. "We have you to thank for maintaining the glorious glow of the city of light, *mes amis*." He steepled his fingers thoughtfully, and I could see Dizzy behind him doing an excellent imitation, to the crowd's delight. "We suspect a small group of cultural radicals to be responsible for these crimes against our city, led by a lunatic pretender to the throne, from a society so secret, they don't even know they exist."

I had to look away to keep from laughing. Then I heard my name. "And to our most welcome visitor, Mademoiselle Mac from California, we present the Pomme Verte, the highest honour possible for a non-French citizen, for her part in preserving the city of light and our most beloved monument, Notre Dame de Paris."

I was nudged forward and onto the stage to accept my green apple, feeling a little like I was at the school field day awards ceremony. I thanked everyone I could think of, from Sashay to Jerome, Rudee, of course, and Blag, who was still nowhere to be seen. Someone took a picture of me shaking hands with Magritte and holding the Pomme Verte then disappeared.

The radio over the bar crackled, and Madeleine's voice could be heard over the din of the room. "Bravo, Mac, and now, *mesdames et messieurs*, CAFTA proudly presents, our very own *groupe du jour*, the band with the big borscht beat, the Hacks!"

Again the crowd applauded and whistled as Mink stood up behind his drums and clicked his sticks together. "One two, you know what to do."

The Hacks stormed into their opening number. I think it was "Grasse Matinee," but I'm not sure. The room shook as the crowd danced, clapped, and stomped in time to the music. The stage was tiny but still left room for general wackiness from the band. Mink twirled his sticks like batons as Maurice attempted to lift Dizzy's pork pie hat from his head with his bow. Dizzy was leaning into the crowd and taunting the dancers with the flag on the end of his slide, and even the normally sedate Henri played a banjo solo with his shining teeth. Rudee omitted nothing from his bag of tricks, and all the silliness I'd witnessed alone in the balcony of the Église Russe was now shared with the "partypoppers" at CAFTA.

Mink's big vocal solo was a highlight and featured his lyrical gifts in lines like, "*You pour moi. Me pour toi. What have we got. Je ne sais quoi.*"

Then came a surprise appearance. I don't know where she'd been hiding, but it was with great drama and more than a little pride that Rudee introduced "The most beautiful woman ever to grace the Paris stage, *la reine des rêves*, Sashay D'Or." The room parted for her, clearing a space in front of the stage, and Sashay gave her usual beguiling performance. Although minus the special effects and the smoke machine, the impact was somewhat muted. At the end of her show, she pulled me onto the dancefloor and wrapped me in a replica of the silky white scarf.

The Hacks ended their first show with "Gâteau To Go," and the break immediately saw the arrival of the most amazing collection of desserts I'd ever seen in one place. I was told that the master bakers and pastry makers of Paris, who normally work at night to prepare for the next day, had made a special feast of sweets in thanks to the cabbies. Trays of *gâteau* Saint Honoré were followed by towering displays of Vacherin cake, *tartes au citron*, and chestnut *tortes*. Finally, a *gâteau amande* arrived with glazed strawberries on top in the shape of a taxicab that promptly collapsed and sank into the cake as the crowd cheered its arrival.

I grabbed a jubilant Rudee and whispered in his ear. We packed up a sampling of the sweets, including what was left of the strawberry taxi, and headed for his car, unnoticed by the partiers at CAFTA. I was kidding him about his nose solo. We were laughing and almost didn't see a couple approaching through the tangle of cars.

"Blag! Where have you been?" I was very happy to see him and forgot all about his feud with Rudee.

"Hey, kid. Nice landing on Notre Dame. You gotta licence for that scarf? You know Tawdry, don't you?"

I did. The angular skyscraper of a woman from Shadowcorps smiled sweetly at me. "*Bonsoir,* superstar. Nice to see you again."

What Blag had in the horizontal, Tawdry had covered in the vertical. She was stunning in a luminous black chiffon off-the-shoulder gown, but it was the shoes that really set it off. Black, of course, with heels that seemed to start around my knees in gleaming metallic blue and wrapped in a mile or so of licorice-like ribbon. Blag was in a smart black leather suit, uncharacteristically clean-shaven, and I think I detected a whiff of cologne when he came over to me. "I'm gonna skip the flail at CAFTA. Tawdry and I have a little *soirée* to get to."

He glanced over at her with a stupid grin, and she responded with a pout and some breezy batting of her substantial eyelashes. This worked magic on poor Blag. "I just wanted to give you this." He handed me a clumsily wrapped gift and said, "Go ahead, open up kiddo, a little souvenir."

Inside was a Tonnage T-shirt with "Demolition Dance" written on the back and a picture of an exploding building. "Blag, you're so sentimental," I said, and Tawdry rolled her eyes.

I'd forgotten for a moment about Rudee, who'd held back silently during this exchange. It was Blag who made the first move. "Hey, Daroo, listen. Let's put this thing between us to bed, okay? I don't even remember what started it all in the first place."

"You're right, Blag. Let's let biceps be doggone."

Blag looked stunned at this pearl of wisdom, but Tawdry and I couldn't let it go by and pretended to flex our muscles, giggling. Rudee and Blag began an earnest conversation full of references to the "old country" and seemed to be making up for lost time. Before long they were laughing, and Blag affectionately slapped Rudee's shoulder, almost knocking him over.

Tawdry took a sisterly tone with me. "Listen, honey, you ever wanna ditch those sneakers and get into some heels sometime, I got a starter set I could get you going with."

"Sure, thanks," I said and called to Rudee that we'd better get rolling on our sweets delivery.

Thirty

We pulled up in front of Madeleine's turret office in Montmartre. It was late and the streets were almost empty. The last few parties were slowly dying down in windows above the street. Madeleine's light was still on, so we knocked and went in, climbing the ramp carefully with our arms full of pastries. We could hear that she was listening in on the CAFTA party, still going strong, on her two-way radio. "Ah, Rudee, Mac, *bonsoir. Quelle fete!*" She indicated the party sounds in the background as she rolled over to meet us.

We relived some of the night's events, and she told us that she'd heard lots of good stories from her chauffeurs who stopped in on their way to CAFTA. "Ah, but you know I don't like crowds, Rudee. And I feel like I'm there, especially with this delivery of yours. *Merci!*" She happily investigated the deserts and zeroed in on the *gâteau amande* with strawberries.

"Madeleine, how did you know to send the cabbies to Notre Dame?" My curiosity couldn't wait.

"Look, *ma petite*." She led me to the screen on her console and hit a couple of buttons. The map of Paris, showing all the cabs currently at one place, CAFTA, zoomed in to the Isle de La Cité. She made another adjustment, and it zoomed in on Notre Dame.

"I was looking for you all over Paris when you disappeared with that horrible smoky man, and finally I found you here."

She shifted the perspective on the screen and caught the giant crane full on then the rooftop of the cathedral. "What's that hanging on the spire?" I asked.

Madeleine arched her brows and gave me a motherly look. "Your special scarf, *ma cherie*. *Très jolie* and very strong. It held you and that crazy man in mid-air until you could be rescued!"

I was speechless. Rudee jumped in. "You saw all this on your screen in 4D?" he asked, sounding shocked.

"Oui. Technology. *C'est magnifique*!" She did a little wheelie and spin in her chariot for emphasis. "Rudee. Time for the Hacks' second show, *non*?"

I thanked her for co-ordinating my rescue, and Rudee and I returned to CAFTA, where the crowd was refusing to give it up for the night. When we got back, many in the room were gathered around the little TV set, waiting for the news coverage of the evening's events. It was still showing highlights of parties around the city when it cut to our windswept reporter, who dramatically related a prime time version of the attempted monument thefts, with no mention of Shadows or gargoyles. Then, to my amazement, the camera panned to her right, and there was Luc Fiat, who with some serious help in the hair and makeup department, didn't look much like his mad brother anymore.

"Yesss. Ouiiii. I think it was the best Bastille Day ever," he commented as they were showing footage of the fireworks and the river rats with their torches, followed by crowds carrying candles and lighters. I could see how it all looked like part of the fun. "It shows the world that Paris does really know how to lighten up!" He laughed gaily at the mention of his beloved campaign.

"But, Monsieur Fiat," Louise attempted to redirect the interview, "what about the unfortunate timing of the power failure? Events all over the city had to be cancelled. It was almost impossible to get around. So much food was spoiled."

"Yes, *oui*, Louise, that's true. By the way, did I mention how flattering those earrings are? They pick up on the colour of your eyes wonderfully." He practically oozed. Before she could bring things back to her question, he continued, "But there is someone I wish to thank especially."

Everyone at CAFTA began calling out my name, and I blushed beet red, as the expression goes. On the screen, Fiat gestured to his left, and the camera panned again, this time to include a grinning face. I couldn't believe who it was — the gluttonous cloud doctor responsible for so much of Louche's mayhem.

"Dr. Etienne Brouillard, the eminent scientist, expert in all matters of light and dark. He was able to sort out the little power problem and to restore the electricity before the night was over. He was also instrumental in locating the missing monuments."

The doctor, who had obviously switched sides overnight, just wasn't ready for his close-up. The camera caught him sliding what looked like a large ox tongue, covered in mayonnaise, down his eager throat. He tried to speak as the light found him, but his mouth was too full to allow any words to come out. Mayo splashed on his coat, and Louise must have directed the cameraman to spare us any more of this sight. "Well, thank you, Dr. Brouillard and the prefect of Paris, Luc Fiat. And to all of you at home, happy Bastille Day."

The CAFTA crowd lost interest in the news coverage and returned to the spirit of the party. "The Hacks. The Hacks! *Encore!*" they shouted.

The band launched into "Stinkbomb Serenade," and the place was jumping once again. It all gets a bit blurry for me at this point. Fatigue had finally started to overcome the excitement of the last couple of days. I remember Rudee lifting me up on stage at one point and insisting I play "Transatlantic Train" on the organ. I guess those piano lessons with my dad must have come in handy, because I vaguely remember faking my way through the song. My last clear recollection is of Rudee leading Sashay onto the dancefloor for a blissful romantic moment, at least for him, I'm sure.

Thirty-One

When I woke up the next morning in my little room with the curved wooden bed in the Église Russe, I truly had no idea where I was for a minute or so. Rain was rattling the roof of the turret and washing the windows in long streaks that seemed to make the colours of the stained glass run together. As I slowly woke up, I realized that I was going home today. I wasn't sure when I had acquired the bandage on my throbbing ankle, but I knew where the injury had come from.

Then I heard laughter from downstairs, and I recognized Rudee's and Dizzy's voices. I lay back down and decided to take my time. I didn't know how I was going to explain my absence on the tour, but I just couldn't worry about it right away. I looked up at all the tiny carved angels on the bookshelf and the bed and smiled a silent thanks.

Somebody had been watching over me in Paris. I finally said goodbye to my hideaway and made my way downstairs to the kitchen, where the two friends greeted me cheerfully. They now felt like old friends.

"Hey, she's back. Good morning, little pillowhead." Rudee grinned.

"Mac, *ça va?*" said Dizzy. "Hey, nice work on 'Transatlantic Train' last night. Maybe you want to sit in for Rudee if the Hacks go on tour. I think Monsieur Daroo's going to be too busy to leave town now."

He shot Rudee a meaningful glance.

"Oh, that's just pork-pie steam, Mac, ignore him. So Sashay wants to see you off. Are you ready to spank the road?"

I packed up my few things. There was still room for my Sashay scarf from the party and my Tonnage T-shirt. I left the "Lighten Up" beret for Rudee. We said goodbye to Dizzy and rolled through the rainy streets one last time. Rudee pulled up in front of the Scarf Museum, and I noticed that they seemed to be making room for a new display in the window.

He handed me a tape of Vladimir Ughoman's "Zamboni Variations," performed by Vlatislav Ughoman on organ. He also attempted to press a small book of special beet and cabbage recipes on me for my mom. "Thanks, Rudee, but I'm pretty sure she has this one. I'll enjoy the music, though. Who's the organist?"

He sighed and paused before replying. "As long as you don't start calling me Vlatislav, I'll tell you. When I arrived in Paris as a child, I thought the immigration man asked where I was staying. He wanted to know my name, I guess. I told him Rue Daru, the little street with the Église Russe on it, and he wrote down Rudee Daroo."

He gave me his most sheepish expression and most lovable. "Anyway," he said brightly, "see you behind the back burner, little Mac."

From the curb, I leaned in his window and said, "It's not *au revoir*, Rudee, it's *eau de cologne*." It was my best attempt at a Rudeeism, and I did get a laugh from him.

I hurried in out of the rain, and Sashay was waiting for me in her lavender boudoir. She had the tea service ready and a plate of madeleine cookies.

After she poured me a cup, she presented me with a tiny silver swan tea set. *Perfect*, I thought. *My gift to Penelope.* "So will you go back to the club, now that the Shadows aren't taking over?" I asked.

"Mmm, I don't know, my little one. I have done my dance so many times now." She gave me the famous pout, but it turned into a smile. "It might be time for something new."

We walked arm in arm through the Marais, wrapped in our scarves, tossed like we didn't care. If anyone thought we were an odd couple, we didn't notice. As we crossed the river, there was Jerome haggling over the price of a set of miniature books of poetry. I said *merci* for all his help and asked him to say goodbye to the river rats for me. "I almost forgot, little *voyageuse*." He handed me the duck's head umbrella. Now my backpack was getting a bit full.

As we approached the Boulevard St. Michel and the place where I was to meet my group, Sashay paused and kissed me twice on each cheek. She whispered that she would see me soon and swept off into the crowd.

I spotted Mademoiselle Lesage on the sidewalk waving her hands in the midst of a group of eleven girls and eleven backpacks, the bus idling nearby. "Ah, there you are, Mac. Now we are all here." She looked at my ankle. "I'm glad that you're getting better, and I'm so sorry you weren't able to join our walking tour." Penelope smiled conspiratorially from the group. Mademoiselle Lesage pressed a book of architectural wonders of Paris into my hands. "Well, even if you didn't get to see them firsthand, you can still learn something."

I climbed into the seat beside Penelope. "I know, I owe you big time. I'm really sorry for missing the tour. You must have had a fantastic time."

Penelope gave me a sympathetic look. "I can't believe that you made it to Paris and didn't see Les Invalides, the Marais, and especially le Bilbouquet, to say nothing of the eye of the beef windows! Was it miserable being with your dad's cab driver friend? What did you do?"

"No, no, he was pretty cool. We didn't do much. Ate, mostly. I should have caught up with you guys, but the days all kind of ran together, and Rudee, my dad's friend, seemed to need the company. Sorry!"

Penelope pulled a copy of *Le Parisien* from her bag and opened it as the bus crossed the Seine. "It's such a shame that you didn't join us for Bastille Day. The Champs Élysées was incredible." Penelope shot me one of her superior looks as she scanned the front page of the paper. I glanced over to see the photo of Magritte presenting me with the Pomme Verte above the story of my exploits on the roof of the cathedral. "Scarves suit you more than I would've thought. Here," she said, handing me the paper. "I've already read this."

Thirty-Two

On the way home from the airport, I reconstructed a severely edited version of my week of architectural highlights for my dad. I told him that Rudee had been an excellent tour guide to a whole other side of Paris. Details of the Hacks' Bastille Day show brought much laughter. "They're still playing 'Stinkbomb Serenade'? And Dizzy's back in the band. Wow! And I can't believe you met the legendary Sashay. What a week. Did you get any sleep?"

I was investigating the fridge for non-beet snacks when Dad called out, "Hey, I think that's your mom."

Her car door slammed in the drive, and we went to meet her. "Hi honey, how was Twigs and Roots?" my dad asked, hugging her.

"Good, very calming. Mac, I want to hear all about Paris — every last detail. Mmmm, you smell like lavender," she said with her arms around me.

"I missed you two." She looked at my ankle with concern. "And it looks like all that walking didn't help your little injury."

She didn't look any more blissed out than usual. The phone rang, and my dad headed for his studio. "I don't want to talk to anybody," my mom called to him. I could hear him laughing loudly. "I came home a bit early. This afternoon there was going to be a lecture called 'Paper or Plastic,' about materialism. I couldn't do another Triconasana pose if my life depended on it. I want real coffee, now!"

I grabbed her yoga mat and bag from the car as she picked up the stack of unopened mail. "Hey, you'll never guess who that was," my dad said, smiling broadly.

"I don't know, the Pope?" offered my mom.

"Almost as unlikely. Rudee Daroo calling from Paris."

I tried to mask the panicky feeling that hit me. Surely, he wouldn't ...

"He asked me to say a special hello you," he said, looking at me. "Mademoiselle Mac as he called you ... and he and Sashay, the love of his life, are finally getting married! To use his expression, he says he's happy as pig. I can't believe it. The wedding's New Year's Eve in Paris. How does that sound, honey?"

He gave my mom that romantic grin I've seen many times before, and she gave him one right back. "The invitation's for the three of us. What do you think, Mac, would you like to return to the city of light?"

Mac's Guide to Paris

All of the architectural wonders described in this book exist in the city of Paris. Oddly enough, the most famous Parisian monument, La Tour Eiffel, or the Eiffel Tower to English speakers, doesn't figure into the story. But plenty of other beautiful structures feature prominently, from the Gothic masterpiece, the Cathédrale Notre Dame, where the story's wild climax takes place, to the lesser known Russian church where Rudee, one of the main characters, lives.

When Mac first arrives in Paris, she meets one of the *bouquinistes*, the booksellers whose stalls line the river Seine on both sides. While not known for their appearance, the book stalls are a longstanding presence in the city and are great places to find unexpected treasures and meet some truly interesting local characters. Parisians are very proud of their historic city, and Jerome, the bookseller Mac meets, is no exception. He points out the beautiful Pont Neuf, one of thirty-seven bridges that cross the river throughout the city, and remarks upon the fact that the "new bridge," as the name translates from French, is in fact one of the oldest in the city. Mac is taken with the bridge even in a downpour, and it's a location she returns to in a very dramatic scene later in the book. If you look at the statue of Henry IV, you'll see that his horse's hooves are in the air. Legend has it that this means that the rider died in battle; if the hooves are on the ground, the rider died in bed or perhaps in the middle of a high-calorie feast.

The first stop on what will prove to be a very eccentric tour of the monuments of Paris is at the Église Russe, the Russian church where Rudee lives and plays the organ. While Rudee and the composers whose music he loves are fictional, the church, located on a quiet street in the 8th arrondissement of Paris, is real and very beautiful. And, yes, Picasso did get married there to a Russian ballerina, Olga Khokhlova!

Mac's school group is staying in the 5th arrondissement, in an area known as the Latin Quarter. It's one of the oldest parts of the city, but home to probably the youngest residents, including the students at the Sorbonne, the city's most prestigious university. The arrondisements, by the way, are the twenty districts that the city is divided into, and if you look at a map you'll see that they're laid out in a spiral, starting with the first arrondisement where the Louvre Museum is located. *Allô*, Mona Lisa!

When Mac comes upon the "Lighten Up!"

festivities, they're taking place on the world's widest boulevard, the fabulous Champs Élysées, in view of the Arc de Triomphe. When you see the arch in photographs, its majestic shape is likely the first thing you notice, and when you read about it, its history as the home to the tomb of the unknown soldier is always mentioned, but to Parisians, the Arc de Triomphe represents something else: one of the worst traffic nightmares in all of Paris! If you're a local, it's called *l'étoile*, which means "the star," because if you look at it from above, the streets leading to the arch look like a star. The drivers, and especially the taxi drivers, seem to treat this roundabout as an opportunity to drive as fast and furiously as humanly possible so they can get on with the business of pursuing the next café au lait!

The first of many architecture-related crimes that Mac sees in the story takes place at the domed church at Les Invalides, a vast military museum commissioned by Louis IV, the "Sun King," that does contain the tomb of Napoleon Bonaparte, who is buried in six coffins, one inside the other. The golden dome of the church is visible from many places around Paris, and happily, the greatest concern that Parisians have for it is the expense of having it repainted!

Les Halles is an area of Paris that housed a huge marketplace from about the twelfth century until the early 1970s, when it was torn down. The market did move, but not underground as it does in our story.

Gargoyles figure prominently in the story and have a long history in France and elsewhere. They are often carvings of mythological creatures found on the edges of buildings and at one time, before drainpipes were common, they served the purpose of diverting water from the sides of the buildings. Gargoyles, like the grotesque-looking ones on the Notre Dame Cathedral, were thought to scare people into attending church!

The Place de la Bastille is one of the most important landmarks in all of France. It represents the place of origin of the French Revolution. The golden "Spirit of Freedom" statue remains atop the July Column, balanced delicately on one foot. On Bastille Day, celebrations featuring fireworks, parades, and concerts take place all over the country and around the world.

The Paris underground, or catacombs, is a maze of hundreds of miles of tunnels, originally mined for the stone that made buildings like the Louvre and the Cathédrale Notre Dame. Right beneath the streets, all sorts of strange wonders are revealed: graffiti from the French Revolution; bunkers that hid everyone from the Nazis to the members of the French Resistance in the Second World War; the leftovers of all-night rave parties; and indeed, stacks of bones from over 1,200 years ago up to the Revolution. You can visit the sewers officially, but most of the underground is forbidden to explore, although many do.

The Cathédrale Notre Dame is one of the jewels of Paris, a shining example of Gothic architecture, built beginning over eight hundred years ago. Lots of royalty have been married and buried here, and the Victor Hugo novel *The Hunchback of Notre Dame* is set there. One brave fellow walked on a tightrope between the two towers. Not encouraged by the authorities!

Fun with Names

Dr. Brouillard: *Brouillard* is the French word for fog.

Blag: The word *blague* in French means "joke."

Luc Fiat: A reference to the phrase from the Bible, *fiat lux*, which means "let there be light."

Louche is a French word meaning "shady."

Magritte: He's the easily distracted detective in this book, but his namesake, René Magritte, was a beloved Belgian Surrealist painter known for his whimsical images of raining men and his love of green apples.

Maurice and Henri Rocquette: *Roquette* is French for arugula. The brothers' names refer to the famous

Canadian hockey-playing Richard brothers. The elder, Maurice, was known as "The Rocket."

Rudee Daroo: The street that the Russian church is located on is Rue Daru.

Acknowledgements

Thanks to the Clows — Anna, Simon & Funmi — for the best of times in Paris, Stephen Stohn, Allister Thompson, Michael Carroll, Courtney Horner, and Marian Hebb.

More Great Novels from Dundurn

Eldritch Manor
by Kim Thompson
978-1459703544
$12.99

Twelve-year-old Willa Fuller is convinced that the old folks in the shabby boarding house down the street are prisoners of their sinister landlady, Miss Trang. Only when Willa is hired on as housekeeper does she discover the truth, which is far more fascinating.

Eldritch Manor is a retirement home for some very strange beings indeed. All have stories to tell — and petty grievances with one another and the world at large.

Storm clouds are on the horizon, however, and when Miss Trang departs on urgent business, Willa is left to babysit the cantankerous bunch. Can she keep the oldsters in line, stitch up unravelling time, and repel an all-out attack from the forces of darkness ... all while keeping the nosy neighbours out of their business and uncovering a startling secret about her own past?

The Time Thief
by Angela Dorsey
978-1926607276
$9.99

One evening as twelve-year-old Mika walks to her friend Aimee's house, she hears a cat yowl and goes to rescue it in front of an abandoned house. She brings the cat home and decides to call her Angel. With Angel safe at Mika's home, strange things start to happen. Someone appears to be watching the house, and a dark presence seems to stalk her in the woods.

One day after school Mika arrives home to find that Angel has disappeared. Mika is broken-hearted and worried for the gentle little cat. When Mika and Aimee go out to find Angel, they find her trying to scratch her way out of the house where Mika found her. They free her, but not before Angel's mysterious owner sees them. After a narrow escape, Mika thinks the problem is solved. But then one of her brothers goes missing. Does Mika have the courage to save both her brother and Angel? Or will the darkly gifted, cruel woman claim them all?